Praise for

Campus Cravings

I loved how Lynne was able to tell this story of a man who searched for a decade for his big brother. That in itself was enough to grab my attention and hold it... She did a fantastic job with this book.
~ *Mrs Condit Reads Reviews*

I really enjoyed this addition to the series. I liked both Zeke and Reid and loved revisiting with Kade and his partner, Lark. I thought Ms. Lynne did a great job at allowing these characters to continue to grow and develop into stronger men as the book continued...the chemistry between Zeke and Reid was sizzling hot!
~ *Top 2 Bottom*

I0542320

Good-Time Boys
Sonny's Salvation
Garron's Gift
Rawley's Redemption
Twin Temptations
It's a Good Life

Cattle Valley Volume One
All Play & No Work
Cattle Valley Mistletoe

Cattle Valley Volume Two
Sweet Topping
Rough Ride

Cattle Valley Volume Three
Physical Therapy
Out of the Shadow

Cattle Valley Volume Four
Bad Boy Cowboy
The Sound of White

Cattle Valley Volume Five
Gone Surfin'
The Last Bouquet

Cattle Valley Volume Six
Eye of the Beholder
Cattle Valley Days

Cattle Valley Volume Seven
Bent— Not Broken
Arm Candy

Cattle Valley Volume Eight
Recipe for Love
Firehouse Heat

Cattle Valley Volume Nine
Neil's Guardian Angel
Scarred

Cattle Valley Volume Ten
Making the Grade
To Service and Protect

Cattle Valley Volume Eleven
The O'Brien Way
Ghost from the Past

Cattle Valley Volume Twelve
Hawk's Landing
Shooting Star

Cattle Valley Volume Thirteen
Confessions
Shadow Soldier

Cattle Valley Volume Fourteen
Alone in a Crowd
Second Chances

Cattle Valley
Finding Absolution
Fingerprints and Muddy Feet

Poker Night Volume One
Texas Hold Em
Slow Play

Poker Night Volume Two
Pocket Pair
Different Suits
Full House

Bodyguards in Love Volume One
Brier's Bargain
Seb's Surrender

Bodyguards in Love Volume Two
I Love Rock N Roll
Taming Black Dog Four

Bodyguards in Love Volume Three
Seducing the Sheik
To Bed a King

Seasons of Love Volume One
Spring

Seasons of Love Volume Two
Summer
Fall

Seasons of Love Volume Three
Winter

Brookside Athletic Club Volume One
I'll Stand By You
Soul Restoration

Neo's Realm Volume One
Liquid Crimson
Blood Trinity

C-7 Shifters
Alrik
Seger

Buck Wild
Cowboy Pride
Cowboy Rules

Healing Doctor Ryan
Moor Love
Highland Gaymes
Stolen Memories
Corporate Passion
Dalton's Awakening

Reunion
Sunset Ridge
Broken Colour
A New Normal
Dead Man Living
Seeing Him

CAMPUS CRAVINGS
Volume Eight

Watch Me

Coming Clean

CAROL LYNNE

Campus Cravings Volume Eight
ISBN # 978-1-78184-769-5
©Copyright Carol Lynne 2014
Cover Art by Posh Gosh ©Copyright 2014
Interior text design by Claire Siemaszkiewicz
Totally Bound Publishing

Published in 2014 by Totally Bound Publishing, Newland House, The Point, Weaver Road, Lincoln, LN6 3QN, United Kingdom.

Totally Bound Publishing is an imprint of Total-E-Ntwined Limited.

WATCH ME

Dedication

To my new editor, Stacey. I've loved you as a friend, now I get to extend those feelings to you as my new editor. Fantastic!

Chapter One

Zeke Straus stared up at the neon Clean Slate sign and shook his head. It was a typical gay bar in a typical college town. Unfortunately, he was out of money, again. He glanced at the newspaper in his hand. Finding a job as a bartender had never been a problem for him, thank God. His looks and attitude had always landed him the primo Friday and Saturday night shifts even if the bar already had a regular bartender. Needless to say, he was used to a hostile work environment between him and the rest of the staff.

Zeke never gave a shit if people liked him. The important thing was making as much money in tips as possible so he could move on. He stepped inside the bar and called out. "Hello?"

While he waited for an answer, he studied the place. He took back what he'd thought earlier. The interior of Clean Slate was nothing like the dives he'd worked in previously. Classy was the word that came to mind. "Hello?"

"Just a minute," a deep voice called from the back.

Several minutes later, a gorgeous young blond appeared. He was closely followed by an older, muscular guy, dressed in an old pair of jeans and a white Clean Slate T-shirt. The smile on the blond's face made Zeke wonder if sex was a condition of employment. Not that he minded. He was used to giving the boss man a taste of what he had to offer. He got a good look at the older man and decided he wouldn't mind taking him for a ride at all. Fuck, the man was built. He could do without the short gray and black spikey hair that stuck up at odd angles, but everyone needed at least one flaw. Zeke had one testicle that hung a little lower than the other or else he'd be perfect. God didn't like total perfection, so he always had to give something for people to obsess over.

"I'll see you tomorrow night," the little blond said, holding several new white T-shirts.

Zeke waited for the blond to leave before approaching the sexy boss. "I'm here about the bartender position," he announced.

The man looked Zeke up and down. "I'm Reid Jackson, co-owner of Clean Slate."

Zeke shook Reid's hand. Zeke couldn't get over the size of Reid's paw as it swallowed his hand. "Zeke Straus, just a man looking for a job."

Reid grinned. "Well then, let's see what you've got."

Zeke inwardly groaned as he reached for the fly on the best pair of jeans he owned. His zipper was halfway down before Reid held up a hand to stop him. "I'm flattered, but I meant make me a drink," Reid clarified.

With no embarrassment whatsoever, Zeke zipped up. "Okay." He headed around the bar. "What'll you have?"

"Make me a margarita, a cosmo, a dirty Martini and a Long Island iced tea," Reid instructed.

With practiced ease, Zeke set about making the drinks in the order they had been given. "So, I take it from looking around that you aren't open yet."

Reid sipped the margarita before nodding his head. "It's good, maybe one of the best I've had." He took another sip before answering Zeke's question. "You're not from around here, are you?"

Zeke set the cosmopolitan on the bar. "Just rode into town yesterday. Why? Does that matter?"

"This place used to be called Fallon's on Fifth until the owner fucked up and tried to kill a college kid. It sat dormant for months until after Fallon's trial. My old college roommate, Alec Demakis, called me up and suggested I come to town and check it out. That was two months ago, and, to finally answer your question, yes, we open tomorrow night." Reid tasted the cosmo. "You're good."

"Yep," Zeke agreed. While he finished the last drink on the list, he caught Reid staring at him with a furrowed brow. "Is there a problem?"

"You're small." Reid dragged a hand through his short dark hair. "We're hoping, with the new name, we won't have trouble with the locals, but you never know."

Zeke wanted to point out that five-eight wasn't exactly small, but, comparing himself to the man on the other side of the bar, he guessed he could see why Reid thought it was. "I can hold my own in a fight if that's what you're worried about." Hell, he'd fought off drunk bastards for years.

"I've already hired two security guys, and I hope to add a few more to the payroll. But, yeah, I guess I'm worried about someone giving you trouble."

Zeke leaned against the bar. "Like I said, I can take care of myself."

Reid nodded. "Okay, you're hired."

* * * *

Reid was finishing up some paperwork when Alec and Max walked into the office. "Hey," he greeted his old college roommate.

Alec took a seat in the white leather wingback chair and pulled Max into his lap. "Are we ready for tomorrow?"

"I've got a few more positions to fill, but we're good for now." Reid reached across the desk and handed Alec several files. "Those are our newest employees."

Alec started flipping through them one by one.

"Good," Max said, pointing to the file belonging to the blond server Reid had hired. "Jeremy's in one of my classes. I told him to come down and apply, but I wasn't sure he would."

"He doesn't have much experience, but I figured with a face and body like his, most customers will be forgiving until he gets the hang of things." Reid leaned back in his chair. "The only one I'm skeptical about is Zeke Straus. He mixes drinks like he was born to it, but I'm afraid he might be a little too sexy for his own good."

"Straus?" Alec questioned. "Any relation to Kade Straus?"

Reid shrugged. "I have no idea. He said he just rode into town last night."

"I'll have to find out," Alec said. "Kade's a friend who used to live in town. He and his partner moved to Wyoming several years back."

"If he looks anything like Kade, I can only imagine how sexy he is," Max spoke up. He received a sharp slap to his ass and a scowl from Alec. "Not nearly as sexy as you are," Max added.

Reid was used to the dynamics between the pair, so he had a pretty good idea that Max had purposely made the comment. Reid couldn't imagine spanking someone, but to each their own. Alec had never condemned Reid for his particular appetites when it came to sex, so he tried to do the same with the pair across from him. "I don't know what Kade looks like, but Zeke's gonna earn a fortune in tips. I just worry that someone'll try to take things too far and security won't be able to get to him in time."

"Just tell Jude to keep an eye on him for a few days until we see how he handles himself." Alec repositioned Max on his lap. "Max and I'll be here early tomorrow to set out the reserved signs and go over any last minute details you need help with."

"Sounds good." Reid couldn't get Zeke off his mind. When he'd handed Zeke the uniform T-shirts, Zeke had demanded a smaller size and had asked if they could be modified. Thrown off guard, he'd told Zeke as long as the logo showed and his chest was covered he could do what he wanted. He was now regretting that decision.

Alec stood and set Max back on his feet. "If there's nothing else, we're going to take off."

"Yeah, I'm done for the day. I think I'll go upstairs and relax in front of the TV." Reid walked Alec and Max to the front door before locking up. On the way to his upstairs apartment, he called Brody, his manager at the bar he owned in Philadelphia.

"Place 2B," Brody answered.

"How's business?" Reid let himself into his apartment and tossed his keys on the coffee table.

"Booming. I just sent last week's financial report to your inbox. How's the new place?" Brody asked.

"Ready for business. Although the time of year sucks. With classes coming to an end for the summer, half our business will be leaving town." Reid had already planned for less than stellar sales through the summer, but that didn't make it any easier to handle. "At least by the time classes start up again the staff will be trained and ready."

"It'll be a success," Brody told him.

"I hope so." Reid's family thought he was crazy to move across the country to open a bar when he already had a successful one in downtown Philadelphia, but he needed the challenge. Life in Philly had become stagnant both professionally and socially. He couldn't exactly say he'd fucked every available gay man in the city, but damn close.

"Well, I'd better get ready for the crowd," Brody said.

"Make me money." Reid hung up as he headed for the bedroom. A quick shower and a slow jack-off session in front of the TV were all he was in the mood for.

* * * *

With a towel wrapped around his trim waist, Zeke withdrew the phone book from the bedside table. Already flipping through the pages, he sat on the edge of the hotel bed and tried to find his brother's name.

"Shit." He tossed the book beside him on the bed when he came up empty. Falling back onto the mattress, he stared up at the popcorn ceiling. For years he'd followed leads to his brother's whereabouts as he'd worked his way across the country.

After nine years of coming up empty, he was beginning to think it was time to write Kade off forever. Although his search hadn't been constant, the longest he'd ever stayed in one place was a year, and that was only because he'd been tricked into signing a twelve-month lease.

He glanced at the phone book and groaned, realizing he was at the end of a trail. It would help if he knew something about his brother. Kade had been kicked out when Zeke had been barely eight years old. The only thing he could remember about his oldest brother was that he was always working on a piece of shit motorcycle in the backyard and he had the prettiest hair Zeke had ever seen.

Chuckling to himself, Zeke reached up and ran a hand over his closely cropped hair. He'd been the unfortunate member of the Straus family to have inherited his father's curls. Girls had curls, not guys, and the minute he'd left home he'd cut those fuckers off.

He scooted out of his towel to rest his back against the headboard. Staring down at his waxed groin, he ran a finger over the small patch of black ink that decorated the skin above his cock. It had been a stupid thing to do, but he'd been young and dumb and so turned on by the tattoo artist. He'd originally gone in to get '*Continue to search and you will find...*' tattooed on his arm. Unfortunately, after sharing a fifth of whiskey and a good fuck, he'd left with two different tattoos and a sore ass. The ass had recovered before he'd made it to the next town, but the tattoos continued to follow him.

Turning his attention away from his cock, Zeke stared at the door to his room. It was early enough that he could go out, stir up some trouble and still be in bed before midnight. Or, he thought as he kicked his way under the covers, he could stay in and watch television. Not nearly as exciting as blowing some guy on the dance floor, but he might need to stay in town for a while until he found his next lead and getting a reputation for being a slut so early in the game was a bad idea.

Zeke turned on the TV. "It's just you and me tonight, Sherlock."

* * * *

Kade Straus was in the process of turning out the downstairs lights when his phone rang. Rushing to get the call before it woke Lark, he stubbed his toe on the leg of the couch.

"Fuck," he said, picking up the phone.

"Is this a bad time?" Jace asked.

Kade sat down and rubbed his foot. "Stubbed my toe," he told his ex-boyfriend and best friend.

"Ouch."

When Jace said nothing else, Kade started to get suspicious. "Did you call for a reason?"

"Yeah." Jace sighed into the phone. "Sammy got a phone call earlier from Max, and I need to ask you something."

"Okay…" Kade dragged out.

"Do you have a brother named Zeke?" Jace asked.

Shit. Kade hadn't heard that name in years. "My baby brother's name is Zeke."

"Well, I think he's here in town. Alec's business partner hired a guy named Zeke Straus to be the new bartender at Clean Slate."

Kade sputtered, "Wait. What? No way would a member of my family work at a gay bar." Hell, he'd lost his entire family when he'd come out. He rubbed his tightening chest.

"Max said the birth date on the employment application is July twenty-third if that helps. We're going to the opening tomorrow night. I could snap a pic with my phone and send it to you?" Jace offered.

Kade was ashamed to tell Jace it wouldn't do any good. Zeke had been a kid the last time he'd seen him, but the birthday was the same. "Sure," he mumbled.

"You okay?"

With his head swimming and his heart threatening to beat out of his chest, Kade knew there was only one person who could calm him. "Not really, but I think I'll wake Lark up and talk to him."

"I'm sorry. The last thing I want is for this to affect your health."

"My physical health is good right now. So don't worry." Given his HIV positive status and his past experiences with severe depression, Kade was more worried for his emotional health. "I'll call ya tomorrow."

"Cool." Jace hung up.

Kade sat for several minutes before going upstairs. Lark was sound asleep with a book on his chest and his wire-framed glasses dangling from one ear. Kade's chest eased immediately. He smiled and began to undress.

Kade slid under the covers and moved Lark's book to the bedside table before removing his glasses. "Hey, baby?"

Lark's lashes fluttered several times before his eyes opened fully. "What time is it?"

Kade pulled Lark into his arms. "A little after eleven. Max called."

Lark snuggled against Kade's chest. "How're they doing?"

"Good, I guess. He didn't say." Kade took a deep breath. "He called to tell me Reid hired a bartender at Clean Slate with my youngest brother's name and birthday."

Lark pushed himself to a sitting position and rubbed his eyes. "Alec's new club?"

"Yeah." Kade scrubbed his hands over his face. "I didn't wanna believe it at first, but the odds of two men named Zeke Straus born on the same day are pretty slim."

Lark moved to lie on top of Kade. "If it is Zeke, you need to go see him."

Kade tried to distract himself by running his hands down Lark's back to land on his ass. How could he look his baby brother in the eye after the way he'd been forced to leave him? "I don't think I can."

Lark shook his head and kissed Kade's chin. "I know what your family did to you, but I don't think you can blame Zeke."

Kade closed his eyes. "I don't blame Zeke. I guess I'm more ashamed of myself. I'm not sure I can face him."

Chapter Two

By the time Zeke had arrived for work, he'd already jogged five miles and sweated through five hundred crunches. Keeping his body in top form made him more tips in one night than an average bartender earned in a week. Despite having moved around a lot, he took great pride in his job.

Reid was running a dust mop over the polished black-tiled floor when Zeke walked in. "Don't you have people for that?" Zeke asked, taking off his denim jacket.

Reid stopped mopping to stare at Zeke. "Are you sure you wouldn't like a bigger shirt?"

The extra small shirt was perfect in Zeke's opinion, except for the restriction around his arms. "Sorry about the sleeves, but they were too tight."

"The whole damn thing's too small," Reid gestured to the bared skin between the bottom of the shirt and Zeke's super low-rise jeans. "Every time you reach up for a wine glass, you'll be testing fate."

Zeke grinned. He knew exactly how far he could lift his arms over his head before his cock made an appearance. It was all part of the game. "Gotta show the tats."

Reid stared down at the two inked dollar bills snaking out of his waistband. "This isn't a strip club."

"I make my money in tips." He took a step toward Reid. *Fuck.* The man was sexy in jeans and a T-shirt, but he was devastating in a suit. "And I'm very good at what I do." He stood toe to toe with Reid and looked up into those big brown eyes he'd dreamt about the previous night. "Trust me, and I'll make this place the hottest club in town."

Reid started to reach for Zeke but quickly pulled his hand back. "I think we'll do just fine without a strip show.

Zeke could tell Reid was interested, so he decided to push. He ran a hand up under his shirt to rub across his nipples before slowly drawing it down to tuck just inside his pants. "Don't worry, I don't actually strip. It's all about illusion. The possibility that I could is what sends the horny co-eds into a frenzy."

Reid removed Zeke's hand before replacing it with his own. He narrowed his gaze as his middle finger rubbed back and forth across the base of Zeke's cock. "Stop trying to get a rise out of me or you'll be sorry."

"Really?" Zeke palmed the front of Reid's suit pants. "It feels like I'm doing a good job so far."

The front door opened. "I hope I'm not late. I missed the first bus."

Reid removed his hand and took a step back, breaking the contact between them. He turned to address the fresh-faced blond. "You're not late, Jeremy."

"Cool," Jeremy said, obviously breathing easier. "I was so worried."

"If you two will follow me, I'll show you where to clock in." Reid took off toward the back of the club without a backwards glance.

Zeke grabbed his jacket from the bar and followed Jeremy. The kid had a nice ass, but he preferred muscular men like Reid. He licked his lips and wondered how far Reid would've gone with the showdown had Jeremy not interrupted them.

"Zeke! Are you listening to me?" Reid snapped.

Zeke smiled up at his boss. "No, sir, I was too busy looking at the kid's ass."

"Mine?" Jeremy's eyes rounded as he stared at Zeke.

"Yeah. It's cute, just not the size I prefer," he said honestly.

"Leave Jeremy alone," Reid growled.

"Like I said, he's not my size. I prefer my men big and strong."

Reid's nostrils flared slightly. "Time in and get to work. Doors open in an hour."

Zeke stared at Reid until he disappeared. He turned to Jeremy. "No offense, kid, but I've got my sights set on the boss."

Jeremy shook his head. "Oh. Mr Jackson told me yesterday that fraternisation with co-workers wouldn't be tolerated."

Zeke chuckled and slung his arm around Jeremy's shoulders. Almost every club he'd worked at had had the same rule, but it was a paper rule and nothing more. Still, it wouldn't hurt to use it to keep Jeremy away from Reid. "Then I guess I'd better stop fantasizing about Reid fucking me against the bar."

* * * *

Reid stayed out of the bar until it was time for his new friends to arrive. He checked his appearance in the mirror and took a moment to straighten his red silk tie. He prayed the club would be a success, not because he couldn't afford to take the financial loss but because he'd grown to think of the college town as home.

Walking out of his office, he was assaulted by loud pop music. Evidently the DJ was doing his thing. When he rounded the corner, he was surprised to see an empty dance floor. Although most of the tables were full, the place seemed dead. "What the hell's going on?" he asked Alec, taking a seat at a long table. He made sure to sit with his back to the bar. The last thing he needed was the distraction of Zeke's tight body.

Alec shrugged. "People are buying booze. They're just not dancing."

Reid knew from experience that the more people enjoyed themselves, the longer they stayed. "Why don't you get Max out there on the dance floor with you?"

Alec shook his head. "Wrong kind of music for me. You want my ass up there, it'd better be something slow."

Beer in hand, Max leaned forward. "He's a grinder," he told Reid.

Reid chuckled. "Yeah, I remember Alec's dance moves from college."

Jeremy tapped Reid on the shoulder. "Zeke would like to speak to you when you get a minute."

Reid glanced back at the bar. Zeke smiled and nodded as he continued to fill drink orders. "Tell him I'll be there in a second."

Jeremy waved to Max. "Hi, Professor Henley."

"Jeremy," Max returned. "Can you get me another white Russian?"

"Sure thing, comin' up." Jeremy hustled off to the bar.

"He seems to be doing pretty good," Max said.

Reid hadn't noticed, but he agreed to keep the peace. "Yep." Knowing he'd put Zeke off as long as he should, he got to his feet. "Anyone need anything from the bar?"

"I'll take that bartender's phone number if you can get it for me," someone from the next table shouted.

Reid shook his head. Although he didn't say it, there was no way in hell he'd fix Zeke up. Just because he planned to try like hell to resist the sexy little fucker didn't mean he wanted to see him with someone else. Arriving at the bar, he leaned against the glowing blue top. "Whatcha need?"

Zeke grinned. "Everything you've got, boss man."

Reid's cock started to harden at the implication. "Either tell me why you called me over or I'll go back and sit with my friends."

"I've seen several people leave already," Zeke said.

"I noticed that. I think it's the music." Reid tapped his fingers on the bar. "You have a suggestion?"

"Yeah, let me do what I do best," Zeke replied.

"No stripping," Reid warned.

"Promise. Just tell Miguel to play *Single Ladies* by Beyoncé and this place will be lit up before you know it." Zeke winked before going back to his drink orders.

Single Ladies? That didn't even make sense to Reid, but he did as asked. He'd just retaken his seat at the table when the music started. Without turning around, he knew the moment something in the bar changed.

"Oh, fuck," Sam said, scrambling for his phone.

Reid took a deep breath and glanced over his shoulder. There, on top of the bar, was Zeke. Sam had been right. *Oh, fuck.* Zeke was lip-syncing to the song as he gyrated his way down the bar. Shouts and whistles filled the room as the crowd moved toward Zeke.

Alec bumped Reid's shoulder. "They like him."

Reid nodded. His gaze zeroed in on the lower half of Zeke's body. *Christ.* He'd never seen anyone sexier. After adjusting his suit jacket to cover the growing bulge in his pants, he stood. "I'll be in my office." He finished his drink in one gulp. "Tell Jeremy to bring me another Scotch, this time straight up."

* * * *

Zeke felt a hand on his upper thigh and playfully brushed it away. He shook a finger at the man and prayed the others took the hint. He didn't mind showing people what he had, but it was up to him whom he allowed to touch him.

Movement from the VIP table caught his attention. Reid turned from his table and began walking toward his office. Without breaking from the dance, Zeke stared at Reid, hoping the boss man would look at him.

Just before disappearing into the hallway, Reid's gaze landed on Zeke. The intensity of those dark brown eyes made the breath freeze in Zeke's chest. *Touch me*, Zeke silently begged. *I choose you.*

Reid broke eye contact and continued down the hall, leaving Zeke to perform the rest of the song without him.

Zeke returned his attention to the men waving money in the air. He needed to keep his mind on the job, not on Reid. Hell, it was likely that the only reason he wanted his boss was that Reid was obviously playing hard to get.

Zeke got to his knees and allowed the horny patrons to stuff money in the waistband of his low-rise jeans. If Clean Slate proved to be the same as the other bars he'd worked, he'd pack the house with one or two dances a night, and make a hefty sum of money for himself and the club.

* * * *

Kade was in the garage working on his bike when Lark came out of the house. "Hey, I thought you were going to bed?"

"I was, but Sam sent me a video that I think you need to see." Lark turned over a bucket and sat beside Kade. He handed the phone over. "It's Zeke."

Kade held the phone in his palm and stared down at it. "How's he look?"

Lark shook his head. "I don't think you want me to answer that. Just play it."

It had been so many years since he'd laid eyes on his baby brother, Kade wasn't sure he was ready to see the man Zeke had become. His thumb hovered over the phone as the seconds ticked by.

"It's a video, not dynamite." Lark wrapped his arms around Kade's neck and kissed him on the cheek. "Sorry. That was a shitty thing to say. But I know you, and the longer you put it off, the more you'll psych yourself out about it."

Kade blew out a long breath. "You're right." He hit the play button. It took him a few moments to focus on what he was supposed to be seeing as the camera swung wildly around the bar. "Sam sucks as a videographer," he mumbled.

At his first look at the gyrating man on the bar, Kade almost dropped the phone. "That's him?"

"Yeah. I guess everyone in the bar went crazy."

The video wasn't close enough to make out Zeke's facial features, but the provocative way he moved outraged Kade. "Doesn't he know what kind of trouble he can get in behaving like that?"

Lark grinned. "Maybe he needs a big brother to teach him."

The thought of Zeke following the path Kade had taken sent chills through him. Kade kissed the top of Lark's head. "Call Sam and tell him to keep an eye on Zeke. I've got a few things to clean up here before I can leave, but we should be able to pull out of here on Tuesday at the latest."

Lark moved to straddle Kade's lap and began to wiggle. "I love you."

Kade stilled Lark's movements and prayed his partner wouldn't get angry. "I'm sorry, but I'm not in the mood right now."

Lark gave Kade a soft kiss. "Don't apologize. We'll face this together."

The heartbreaking image of a boy running after him as he'd ridden away from his boyhood home had haunted Kade for years. Despite Lark's big heart and willingness to help, Kade knew he was on his own. He was the only one who could exorcise the memory. "Tell Sam we'll leave Sunday morning."

* * * *

Reid looked up when the door to his office opened. He expected to see Jeremy, but was surprised when Alec walked in. "How's it going out there?"

Alec set Reid's drink in front of him. "Great. So what the hell happened to you?"

Reid took a sip. "Did you see Zeke? He's gonna drive me crazy. I've gotta find someone to replace him."

Alec cleared his throat and took a seat in front of Reid's desk. "Lark called Sam. He and Kade are coming up Sunday."

Reid tipped his glass back and gulped the Scotch down. "You don't understand. I'm attracted to him."

"You and every other man in the bar." Alec cleared his throat. "I'd be lying if I said my cock didn't take notice. You're human. Get over it."

Reid set the glass down before running his fingers through his hair. "I've worked around some of the hottest men you'll ever see, and never have I been tempted to break my own rule of not fucking around with my employees." He shook his head. "I've known Zeke for all of thirty-six hours, and I can't think of anything else."

"Okay, so change your rule. It's a stupid one to begin with," Alec said. "You spend your days and nights at work. Hell, you live upstairs. Exactly how else are you supposed to find someone?"

Reid flipped open Zeke's employment folder. "He's worked at eight different clubs in the last two fucking years." He shook his head. "Of all the people I'd break my own damn rule for, Zeke isn't one of them."

"Then I guess you have a problem." Alec stood and buttoned his suit jacket. "If I didn't have Max..." He let his voice trail off and headed for the door. "Fuck him and worry about him staying afterwards."

Reid watched his friend and business partner leave. He thought about Alec's advice and smiled. It was the first time since moving to town that he'd seen a glimpse of the Alec he'd roomed with in college. Max had changed Alec, and although Reid knew it was for the better, he sometimes missed the heartless Dom he'd once known.

Staring down at Zeke's file, Reid wondered why he was hesitating. He'd just gotten the thumbs-up from his business partner. From the way Zeke had been coming onto him, Reid had a feeling he could be balls deep in the man at the snap of his fingers. So, what was holding him back? It wasn't the fear of being hurt. Rarely did he allow someone to get close enough to touch his heart, and he doubted a man like Zeke would be the exception.

A knock sounded at the door a moment before Jeremy stuck his head in. "Alec said you might need another drink?"

Reid noticed the whoops and catcalls had died off in the bar. "Thanks, but I'm coming out." He closed Zeke's file.

Jeremy was still at the door when Reid walked away from his desk. "Is there something wrong?" Jeremy asked.

Reid took off his suit jacket and hung it on the coat tree beside the door. "Nothing another Scotch won't cure." He followed Jeremy back to the bar. Meeting Zeke's gaze, he signaled for another drink.

Zeke slid a glass down the bar toward Reid before grabbing the bottle of Scotch. "I'm glad you decided to rejoin the party."

The front of Zeke's white T-shirt was soaked with sweat, turning the material transparent. Reid felt his cock stiffen as he gazed at the twin dark nipples beneath the fabric. "I needed to think."

Zeke leaned his forearms on the bar, putting himself within inches of Reid. "What about?"

"You," Reid confessed, meeting Zeke's stare.

"And what did you decide?

Reid answered by reaching across the bar and taking one of Zeke's nipples between his thumb and forefinger. He applied enough pressure to get his point across, but not enough to hurt. "I'm still working on it."

* * * *

Zeke handed Jeremy the last tray of drinks for the night. "I'm going to load some glasses in the dishwasher if you need anything."

Jeremy nodded before walking off.

In a hurry to get the bar closed and cleaned up, Zeke carried a bucket of dirty glasses into the kitchen. He heard someone walk in behind him and waited for Jeremy to say something. Instead, strong arms reached around him as a pair of lips began to kiss his neck.

"Mmm," Zeke moaned.

"I thought you'd like that."

Zeke stiffened a moment before he shoved his elbow as hard as he could into a set of ribs. An *oomph* sounded as the man staggered back. Zeke spun around and prepared for a fight. "What the fuck, man!"

Rubbing his chest, the man narrowed his eyes at Zeke. "Don't tell me you didn't want it. You've been flirting with me all night."

Zeke spread his arms out. "I've been flirting with everyone. It's my fucking job, asshole."

When the man came toward him once again, Zeke picked up a glass. "Stop. Do yourself a favor and get the fuck out of here," Zeke told him.

"Or what? You gonna throw that glass at me?" the man asked.

"Throw it. Smash it against your face." Zeke shrugged. "Whatever it takes for you to get the point that I'm not interested."

The man pointed his finger at Zeke. "Don't put it on display if it's not available. You're worse than Jigger. At least he followed through." He spat on the floor before he headed out of the kitchen.

"I'll do whatever the hell I want!" Zeke screamed. He'd had enough of being told what to do.

Zeke heard Reid's raised voice just outside the door a moment before he walked into the kitchen. "What was that guy doing back here?"

"He snuck up behind me and tried to cop a feel," Zeke said, turning to set the glass in the dishwasher rack.

"That surprises me. I'd think you were a little more street-wise than that," Reid replied.

"Yeah, well, I thought it was you." Zeke finished loading the dishwasher before closing the door. He turned around and faced Reid. "How long before this place clears out?"

"Thirty minutes. Forty-five at most." Reid stepped closer, putting his body inches from Zeke's. "Why? You in a hurry to get out of here?"

"Hey, man, we're taking off," Alec said from the doorway.

Reid glanced over his shoulder. "I'll call you tomorrow after I figure the night's take."

Alec smiled at Zeke. "Good job tonight."

"Thanks. It's never a bad thing when you can impress the owner with one dance," Zeke said.

"The dance was nice." Alec rubbed his jaw. "More than nice. But I was referring to your bartender skills. That was the best damn hole in one I've ever been served."

"Glad you enjoyed it, sir." Zeke hadn't formally met Reid's business partner, but it never hurt to get another boss on his side.

"Don't call him sir," Reid ground out between clenched jaws.

Zeke didn't understand Reid's sharp change in demeanor. "Okay."

From the doorway, Alec chuckled. "Night, you two."

Reid stared at Zeke. "Alec's a Dom. I imagine your use of the term 'sir' just made his dick hard."

"I didn't know." Zeke wasn't comfortable with D/s relationships. No doubt it went back to his heavy-handed upbringing. It didn't matter whether he pictured himself doling out the orders or taking them—the idea that he'd willingly put himself in the very position he'd run from made no sense. "Believe me, I won't make the same mistake again."

Reid nodded. "Let's take care of business before we discuss moving on to more enjoyable activities." He leaned down and landed a soft kiss on Zeke's lips. "And make sure, if you're back here alone at night, you lock the door."

"It's a swinging door without a lock," Zeke reminded his boss.

"I'll replace it." Reid gave Zeke another kiss.

Zeke stared up at Reid. "Who's Jigger?"

Reid stiffened. "Where'd you hear that name?"

"My handsy friend said I was worse than Jigger." Zeke crossed his arms over his chest. "So who is he?"

"The bartender who worked here when it was Fallon's on Fifth. He was convicted of raping several customers after slipping GHB and Rohypnol in their drinks," Reid explained.

"I thought you said the owner did that," Zeke said.

"Peas in a pod, only Fallon enjoyed getting rough with his victims." Reid took several steps back. "I told you people in this town wouldn't forget what happened here before, and I meant it. We've got an uphill battle in front of us if we want to make this place thrive."

"And so I dance once or twice a night, depending on the crowd's reaction. I make more money and so do you." Zeke waited. Reid's reaction to his earlier dance hadn't gone without notice, and Zeke refused to work for someone who made him feel like trash. "Well? Do we have a deal or not?"

"I'm not sure why you'd want to do that again after the way that asshole came onto you."

Zeke dug into his back pocket and pulled out the wad of bills he'd earned. "This is why. Over two hundred bucks for one dance, and I didn't even have to flash 'em my cock." He stepped over and took Reid's hand before pressing it against his fly. "This I'll save for you as long as it's in both our best interests to do so."

Reid rubbed Zeke's dick through the denim. "The minute you decide to cheat on me, I'll have you out on your ass."

Zeke grinned. "Don't worry. I'll be long gone before that happens."

Reid's black eyebrows drew together in a scowl. "Breaking my own rules doesn't come easy for me. If you plan to take off in the next couple of weeks, tell me now."

"The only plan I have is finding my brother." Zeke sucked in a breath. In all the years he'd been on the road, he'd never told anyone anything about himself beyond a stupid employment application.

"Is his name Kade?" Reid asked.

Surprised at the mention of his brother's name, Zeke nodded. "How'd you know that?" Gooseflesh covered his arms and chest as he waited for Reid's answer.

"Max, Alec's partner, recognized your name among the stack of employment files I gave them to look over." Reid pointed toward the bar. "That whole group I was sitting with tonight are friends of your brother. One of them contacted him, and he's made plans to drive over here on Sunday."

Zeke's knees threatened to buckle. He staggered over to a stool by the prep island and sat. The day he'd waited twenty years for was within his grasp, and he suddenly wasn't sure how he felt about it.

"You okay?" Reid knelt beside Zeke.

"Yeah." Zeke quickly got himself together and stood. "I'd better get the bar cleaned up." He left before Reid could get to his feet. Jeremy had already cleaned the tables and loaded the glasses in a tub, and Gage, one of the other servers, had already started sweeping.

Reid walked out of the kitchen. "Bring the receipts into my office as soon as you've balanced the register."

"Sure thing," Zeke answered. He regretted that Reid had witnessed his moment of weakness, but hearing the news had rocked him to his soul. *What now?* Realizing his search was finally over left him with a sense of emptiness. Instead of worrying whether or not he'd ever find his brother, he was suddenly left wondering how Kade would react to him.

* * * *

Reid continually tapped his pen on the desk as he stared at the photo of his family. He'd been blessed with a large, loving group of brothers and a dependable father who'd worked his ass off to make sure the family survived. His mother may have left them when they'd been children, but that had just brought them closer. He hadn't been told why Zeke had lost touch with Kade, and he refused to ask. Personal lives should remain personal unless voluntarily exposed.

On a whim, Reid picked up the phone and called information. He eventually obtained Kade's home phone number and chose to spend the extra money to be connected.

"Hello?" a soft male voice answered.

"This is Reid, may I speak to Kade?"

"Oh, hi, this is Lark. Hang on, and I'll find Kade. I think he's out on the porch."

The sound of sheets rustling made Reid wince—he hadn't meant to wake anyone. He heard mumbling and the slamming of what seemed to be a screen door before Kade came on the line.

"This is Kade."

"Hey, it's Reid. I wanted to tell you that I told Zeke that you were coming into town."

"Okay."

Reid picked up his pen and started tapping the desk again. Now he had Kade on the phone, he wasn't sure what to say. He tried to remind himself that he should stay out of the Straus family's business, but Zeke's earlier reaction worried him. "I don't know what's going on between you and Zeke, but I need to make sure you're not coming up to cause trouble for him."

"And just who're you to ask me something like that?" Kade growled.

Good question. Reid rubbed his eyes. "From what I can tell, I'm the only friend he has right now," he finally said.

Kade was quiet for several moments before speaking. "Tell me something, does Zeke seem angry?"

"No." Reid didn't mention Zeke's emotional state when he had found out Kade was coming up to see him. Until he knew what Kade was about and how he would treat his brother, Reid wasn't giving him any more information. "The bar's closed on Sunday, but if you want to give me a cell number, I'll have Zeke call you to set up a place to meet."

"You got a piece of paper?" Kade asked.

"Yep." Reid wrote Kade's number down. "Thanks." Before he could think better of it, he continued, "Thanks for coming up here to meet him. I'm not ready to see him go yet."

"You like my brother?"

"Yes," Reid replied.

Kade made a noise in his throat that Reid wasn't sure how to interpret. "Tell Zeke I look forward to his call."

"Will do." Reid hung up just as the door to his office opened.

"Not bad," Zeke said, handing Reid the bank bag. "I added the credit card receipts on a separate tape because I wasn't sure how you wanted to handle that."

Although he didn't say anything to the contrary, Reid could tell Zeke's mind was no longer on sex. "Unless you're ready to go home, why don't you get us a bottle of Scotch while we go through these?"

"Sure," Zeke said before leaving the office. He was back within minutes with a bottle and an empty glass in one hand and what looked like a Coke in the other.

"You're not joining me?" Reid asked.

"I don't usually drink." Zeke sat on the chair in front of Reid's desk. He tilted his head to the side and studied Reid for several moments. "Do you always drink so much?"

"Only when I'm anxious." Reid slid the piece of paper over to Zeke before filling his glass. "That's Kade's cellphone number. Since we'll be closed on Sunday, you'll have to call him to arrange a place to meet." He tipped his glass back. "If you want to invite him here, that's fine. I live upstairs, so I can unlock the place for you."

Zeke shoved the paper in his jeans pocket. "I'll think about it and let you know."

Reid glanced down at the pile of cash and charge card receipts. "I think I'll take this upstairs and put it in my safe for tonight. Do you want to come up for a while?" It was obvious that the sexual tension between them had cooled a bit, but that was no reason they couldn't get to know each other. "No expectations. I don't know about you, but I'm always too wound up to go to bed right away. I think I'll make some pasta and drink a glass of wine. Maybe watch a little TV. Interested?"

It took Zeke a moment, but eventually he nodded. "Yeah, I'd like that."

Chapter Three

"You like garlic?" Reid asked.

Zeke grinned. "Bring it on." He rubbed his thumb against the piece of paper Reid had given him earlier. Kade was a phone call away. "I can't believe he's going to be here in less than thirty-six hours."

Reid glanced up from his chopping block. "You mind if I ask what happened between the two of you?"

Zeke shrugged and returned his attention to the phone number. "Nothing really happened between us. Kade and my dad never got along, but once he turned eighteen and informed my folks that he was gay, Dad kicked him out. Kade punched Dad in the face and took off on his motorcycle." He remembered the day like it was yesterday. "I was in the yard when he climbed on his old bike and told me 'Later'." Zeke looked at Reid. "That was it. I didn't know at the time I'd never see him again." He swallowed around the lump in his throat. "Once I graduated, I made it my mission to find him."

Reid set the knife down and wiped his hands on a dish towel before walking over to the island. "And you've been looking for him ever since?"

Zeke nodded. "That's why my employment record looks like it does."

Dinner obviously forgotten, Reid slid onto a stool beside Zeke. "What'll you do now that you've found him?"

"I don't know." Zeke ran his fingers through his hair. Reid was easy to talk to, something he hadn't really found with anyone before. "I've lived the last ten years for my brother. I'm not sure where to go from here." He took a deep breath. Enough of the pity party. "I'll figure it out. I always do."

Reid leaned in and kissed Zeke. It was a soft, questioning kiss that Zeke immediately responded to. He grabbed the back of Reid's neck and held him close as he opened his mouth for Reid's tongue. Fuck, Reid could kiss. Zeke felt his body begin to heat at the erotic play of tongues and lips.

Groaning, Zeke climbed off his stool without breaking their connection and insinuated himself between Reid's spread thighs. When he'd come upstairs, he'd put thoughts of sex on the back burner, but, damn, if Reid's kiss lit him up, what would feeling their naked bodies entwined do? Shit, Zeke couldn't even imagine.

Reid rested his hand on Zeke's ass and squeezed as he pushed his other hand up underneath Zeke's tight T-shirt.

When Reid began to pinch and scrape against Zeke's nipples, he broke the kiss and moaned. "Want you," Reid mumbled, his voice so deep that Zeke barely understood him.

Zeke rubbed his erection against Reid. "Yeah," he agreed. He began to unbutton Reid's dress shirt, amazed at the trimmed pelt of greying hair on Reid's chest. "In here?"

Reid shook his head and got to his feet. "Supplies are in the bedroom." He kept his hand on Zeke's ass and walked them out of the kitchen. The moment they entered the bedroom, Zeke reached for the zipper on his low-rise jeans, but Reid stopped him. "Wait. I'll do that." He pulled Zeke's T-shirt off and threw it to the floor.

Zeke was gently pushed onto the bed with the rest of his clothes still on. He stared up at Reid and wondered what would happen next.

Reid rid himself of his shoes, socks and shirt before loosening his belt.

Zeke suddenly wondered whether Reid was into using that belt on his lovers. Didn't matter if Reid was used to it or not, that was definitely one kink Zeke wasn't into and wouldn't allow. He clasped his hands under his head as he continued to watch Reid.

Reid dropped the belt to the floor before reaching for his zipper. "Have you ever fucked in front of someone else?"

Startled by the question, Zeke wasn't sure how to answer it. "What?"

Reid removed his pants and underwear. He casually reached into the bedside table and removed a bottle of lube and a box of condoms. "You seem to like the attention you get when you dance. I was just wondering how far that went?" He ran a hand down Zeke's chest to the deep creases cut into his pelvis above his jeans.

"Are you asking me if I'm an exhibitionist?" Zeke asked, leaning up on his elbows to watch Reid's exploring fingers.

Reid walked around the edge of the bed and yanked Zeke's jeans down farther without unzipping them, baring the base of Zeke's cock. "Yes, that's exactly what I'm asking."

"Well, I've never had sex in front of people, but I guess you could say I enjoy getting men all hot and bothered by teasing them with my body," Zeke confessed. "Why? You have a problem with that?"

"Just the opposite, actually. The reason I left the room when you were dancing was because I couldn't think of anything I wanted more than to stick my hand down your jeans with everyone watching." Reid leaned over and licked the base of Zeke's cock. "Or more."

Zeke unsnapped the button on his jeans and slowly lowered the zipper, revealing more of his hefty cock. He'd fucked against, on top and over a bar, but never during working hours. He admitted to himself that the thought wasn't necessarily unappealing, but it could get dangerous. "If you'd done something like that, everyone in the place would've thought it was okay to stick their hands down my jeans."

"Not if I made it known that they could look but not touch," Reid countered. He sat on the edge of the bed and slowly freed Zeke's cock. Holding the heavy length in his hand, Reid shook his head. "Give me exclusive free access to your body while you're in town, and I'll treat you like a king."

Zeke toed off his boots and let them fall to the floor. "I don't know how long I'll stay," he reminded his boss.

"I know." Reid swiped his tongue across the crown of Zeke's cock. "But I'd love the chance to get to know you better while you're here."

Zeke thought about Reid's offer. He wasn't being promised love and romance, which was a good thing. Hot sex and an enjoyable way to spend the next few weeks making money was a pretty damn good offer. He'd run across men before who enjoyed the danger of fucking in public places, but Zeke had never been interested. So why was he entertained by the idea of doing it now? Reid took that moment to engulf the entire head of Zeke's cock and about half of his length. *Fuck, yeah.* "No groping around my brother," he informed Reid.

Reid nodded without taking Zeke's cock from his mouth.

"And touching is fine, but I'm not ready to be fucked in front of a bar full of people," Zeke clarified.

Reid released Zeke's cock and pushed Zeke's jeans down and off. "I'd never let it go that far. My office with the door open, maybe, probably, but not right out in the main bar."

Zeke grabbed the lube and held it out. "Show me exactly what I'll be getting in your office?"

Reid took the bottle. "Back or knees?"

"I've just worked a long shift, I'll stay on my back," Zeke replied, spreading his legs and planting his feet on the mattress.

Not the least bit shy of showing off his body, Reid knelt on the bed. He grabbed his cock by the base and stroked himself several times before slapping his length against Zeke's thigh. "Wider."

Zeke hooked his forearms under his knees and brought his legs closer to his chest, exposing his hole to Reid's gaze. "Better?"

"Infinitely." Reid released his cock and poured lube onto his fingers. It was hard to tell how long it had been for Zeke, and he figured it would be rude to ask, so he decided to play it by ear. He circled Zeke's puckered hole several times before dipping the tip of his finger inside. "Fuck, I know what I said, but I can just imagine you spread out like this on the bar downstairs."

"Maybe one of these nights after closing." Zeke groaned when Reid inserted a finger and began drawing it in and out of his hole.

Reid liked the idea of Zeke sticking around for a while. It had been quite a while since he'd found a partner who would let him indulge in his particular kink. He added more lube to Zeke's hole before inserting another finger. "Hand me a condom, would ya?"

Zeke released one of his legs and reached for the box. "You've only got three left."

"I'll get some more tomorrow." Reid took the foil packet and ripped it open with his teeth. If he had his way, they'd use all three rubbers in the next few hours. He rolled the condom down his length before pouring a generous amount of lube into the palm of his hand. After scissoring his fingers several times, he leaned down and licked the tip of Zeke's cock. "You ready?"

"Oh, yeah." Zeke rested his heels on Reid's shoulders and scooted closer until he could drape his legs down Reid's back. With his hands free, he reached between his legs and started stroking his cock. "How many bartenders have you fucked like this?"

Reid didn't let the question slow him down. He guided the tip of his cock to Zeke's stretched hole and slowly pressed in. It wasn't until he was fully buried inside Zeke's warmth that he finally spoke. "I've never fucked an employee, if that's what you're asking. Though I have had my fair share of bartenders over the years."

"Damn, that's crazy. Have you had ugly people working for you in the past or what?"

Reid assumed that if Zeke was able to form full sentences, he wasn't doing his job right. He decided to fix that. Without warning, he pulled out before slamming his cock in deep. A gasp from Zeke was music to Reid's ears. He began a punishing rhythm in and out, changing angles often in order to keep Zeke off balance.

After a good ten minutes of hard fucking, Reid pulled out, and tapped Zeke's hip. "Roll over."

The second Zeke's ass was back in the air, Reid drove his cock in hard, slapping his sac against Zeke's in the process. "Great ass," he growled.

"Great cock," Zeke returned.

Reid couldn't help but grin. He found himself wanting to know more about the man he was fucking. Did he like sports? Was he a fan of trash TV or did he enjoy old movies like Reid did?

He shook his head. Why the hell was he thinking about bullshit like that when he had a sexy tight ass wrapped around his cock?

Zeke cried out, signaling his release just as he clamped down around Reid's cock.

"Fuck," Reid panted. He gritted his teeth and tried to ride out Zeke's orgasm without coming. Slowly,

Zeke relaxed, giving Reid the room he needed to begin fucking him again. When Zeke sagged to the mattress, Reid followed him, still pistoning in and out of him.

A few minutes later, Reid slammed in for the last time and erupted, filling the condom. His entire body seemed to spasm as he emptied his balls. "Shit."

Zeke allowed Reid to lie on him for several moments before eventually elbowing Reid in the ribs. "Can't breathe."

Reid reached between them and secured the condom as he pulled out of Zeke's ass. He rolled over onto his back and stared at the ceiling as he reached blindly for a tissue on the bedside table. The encounter had shaken him and he couldn't put his finger on the reason. It was just a fuck. No feelings had passed between them, no words of love or promises of forever, so why the hell did he feel like pulling the covers over them and keeping Zeke in his bed for the next twenty or thirty years?

Motherfucker!

* * * *

After a short nap, Zeke woke to the smell of garlic. "Mmm." His stomach rumbled, reminding him that he hadn't eaten since lunch. He looked at the clock and chuckled. Only someone who was used to working in a club could eat pasta at four in the morning. He swung his legs over the side of the bed and got to his feet.

He stared down at his jeans and decided against putting them on. With high hopes of getting fucked again after dinner, Zeke wandered out of the bedroom. "Smells good."

Standing at the stove wearing nothing but an apron, Reid glanced over his shoulder. "I wasn't sure whether or not to wake you."

Zeke shuffled over to Reid and gave him a deep kiss. "I'm so hungry that the smell of food woke me."

Reid reached down and gave Zeke's flaccid cock a soft caress. "The sauce is ready. I just need to put the pasta in the pot."

Zeke draped his arm over Reid's shoulder and kissed him again while Reid continued to play with his cock. He tasted garlic and bell peppers as he lapped at the inside of Reid's mouth. Breaking the kiss he moaned. "You taste good."

"I'm glad you think so. For a minute there I thought you were gonna eat my tongue."

Zeke nipped Reid's chin with his teeth. "Don't tempt me."

"I'd better feed you before things get dangerous." Reid gave Zeke's half-hard cock one more squeeze before releasing it. "Give me five minutes. I just need to get this pasta in the pot."

Zeke stepped back to give Reid room. He hated the way he felt without Reid's touch. Hated it because it meant he was becoming attached. It wasn't that he'd never experienced the feeling before, but it had always ended when he'd moved on. *No, I'm not going there.* He turned and wandered into the living room.

The room was very modern in design, which could've easily translated to being cold, but Reid had warmed the space with a large deep blue rug and dozens of photographs. He studied the pictures. "Your family?"

"Huh?" Reid asked from the kitchen.

Zeke carried one of the framed photos into the kitchen. "Are these all brothers?"

Reid glanced over his shoulder. "Yeah, all five of us." He gave the colander one last shake over the sink before pouring the pasta into a large dish. He added the sautéed vegetables and topped the whole thing off with freshly grated Parmesan cheese.

Zeke moved the photograph to the side to make room for the pasta. "So are you all still pretty close?"

Reid tossed his apron on the counter. He held up the bottle and waited for Zeke's approval of the wine choice before continuing. "I talked to them every couple of weeks. I call my dad three or four times a week to check in and he usually fills me in on every detail of their lives, so…" He poured two glasses.

Zeke couldn't take his eyes off Reid's cock as it bounced toward him. For a man in his forties, Reid was still fucking amazing.

Reid sat beside Zeke. "What about you? You have family other than Kade?"

Zeke took a sip of wine. "Isaiah's six years older than I am. He's a stock broker, if you can believe it."

Reid dished pasta onto their plates. "Do you keep in touch with him?"

"I give him a call a couple times a year. He has his own life." Zeke didn't say more because there wasn't much else to be said. Isaiah didn't seem to like Zeke, which was mutual. He glanced at the picture again, wondering what it would be like to have a perfect family. *Forget it*, he told himself, knowing what-ifs always depressed him. He took his first bite of dinner and moaned in appreciation. "This is good."

Reid reached over and wrapped his hand around Zeke's cock as he continued eating. "I cook almost every night after I get off work. You're welcome to join me anytime."

Zeke struggled to concentrate on his food as Reid began to stroke him. It was nearly four thirty in the morning, yet he couldn't have been more awake. He was used to ducking out as soon as the fucking was over, but he found himself wanting to stay, hoping for another round, or two—okay maybe three or four if he was totally honest with himself. *Shit.* He might be in trouble.

* * * *

Reid was busy filling out the deposit slip when his phone rang. "Hello?" he answered without looking at the display.

"How was your opening?" Rick, Reid's younger brother, asked.

"Good, but what else did you expect. I've told you, baby boy, I've got the golden touch in the family." Reid chuckled.

"Remind me again where it is you live? Oh, wait, you live above a bar," Rick shot back.

"A bar that I own instead of living in a huge five thousand square foot house that I can't afford to furnish," Reid returned. It was a typical exchange between the brothers. One that Reid had come to rely on.

"I've got the money to furnish it, but why should I? I live in the TV room and the bedroom."

"You need a wife." Reid grinned. He knew Rick's typical response was coming in three…two…one—

"And deprive the rest of the men and women in Philadelphia? Forget it."

"Somehow I knew you'd say that." Reid had three heterosexual brothers and one bisexual brother and not one of them was married. They didn't discuss it, but Reid knew it went back to the way their mother had left them and their father.

"What about you? You gettin' some action in Bumfuck, Idaho?"

"Maybe." Reid shifted in his chair.

"Maybe? What the fuck's that mean?"

"It means you need to mind your own business and stay out of mine, asshole." There was no sting to his words. Reid knew his brother wouldn't take offense.

Rick whistled. "Must be someone special. You're usually bragging about your conquests by now."

"Can we talk about something else? How's Dad?" Reid heard a knock at the door. "Come in." He couldn't wipe the smile off his face when Zeke walked into his office. He covered the mouthpiece with his palm. "My brother Rick," he said and gestured to the phone.

"Is someone there?" Rick asked.

"Yeah, but tell me how Dad's doing? Last time I talked to him he mentioned he'd had trouble with his blood sugar levels." The fact that Reid had gotten the information out of his father was a total fluke. Usually his dad didn't want to talk about himself, preferring to know every detail of his sons' lives.

"Okay, I guess. Aaron took him for his regular appointment on Thursday. I'm sure if something was wrong, Aaron would at least tell us."

Zeke pointed toward the door. *"You want me to leave?"* he mouthed.

Reid shook his head and cleared the desk in front of him. He moved his chair back and patted the top of the desk.

With a wicked grin, Zeke settled on the desk.

"Why'd you let Aaron take him? We all know he's as bad as Dad when it comes to revealing shit." It was hard to concentrate on his conversation with Zeke so close, but he wouldn't have it any other way. The thought both scared and delighted him. How long had it been since a lover had so fully captured his attention?

"Dad asked Aaron to take him, but I really don't think Aaron would hide something from us," Rick said.

Reid tucked the phone between his ear and shoulder to free both hands. He immediately went for the button on Zeke's jeans. There wasn't time before the club opened to fuck the man like he wanted, but he could at least send Zeke out in front of all those young studs completely satisfied. "I hope not," he replied to his brother.

Reid stuck his hand in Zeke's jeans to shield his cock as he lowered the zipper. "The club'll open soon, so I need to get off here, but let me know immediately if you find out anything."

"I won't, but you know I'll call if anything comes up."

"Thanks. Love you." Reid leaned in and ran his tongue up the length of Zeke's erection.

"You, too," Rick said before hanging up.

"Hang that up for me, will ya?" Reid asked Zeke a moment before engulfing the head of Zeke's cock into his mouth.

Zeke moaned. "Keep that up and I'll do anything you ask." The handset was almost to its cradle when Zeke stopped and put the phone to his ear. "Hello?"

Reid released Zeke's cock and froze.

A wide smile on his handsome face, Zeke nodded. "Yeah." He nodded again and gave Reid a thumbs-up. "Bartender. Yep. Well he was sucking my cock until you decided to eavesdrop."

Reid reached for the phone, but Zeke lay back, putting it out of reach as he continued to talk to Rick. "Hell yeah, he's fucking fantastic at it, but don't you think it's kinda sick that you're asking how well your brother gives head?"

Mortified, Reid got to his feet and grabbed the phone. "Hang the fucking phone up, Rick," he growled into the receiver.

Rick was laughing his ass off on the other end when Reid slammed the phone down, disconnecting the call. "I can't believe you told him that." Reid leaned over to lay his upper body on top of Zeke's. "He'll use that against me for the rest of my life."

Still grinning, Zeke wiggled his hips. "I can't believe he had the balls to ask how talented your mouth is. That's a sick fucker."

Reid couldn't disagree. "Yeah, but he's a good guy otherwise." He reached between them and squeezed Zeke's cock. "We didn't get much sleep. You sure you're okay to work?" he asked, trying to change the subject.

"I'll be fine. I took a short power nap before coming back in." Zeke pulled Reid's head down for a deep kiss.

The kiss fired Reid up within moments. He was reaching for the zipper on his own jeans when another knock sounded at the door. Reid broke the kiss and stared down at Zeke. "Want me to get up?"

Zeke shook his head.

"Come in," Reid called, still lying on top of Zeke.

"I just wanted..." Holt, one of Clean Slate's bouncers, broke off when he spotted Reid and Zeke. "Oh, sorry."

"That's okay." Reid stood and readjusted the hard cock in his jeans without taking his hand off Zeke's cock. It was his first chance to stake his claim, and he wouldn't let the moment pass, especially with someone as good-looking as Holt. The bouncer stood at least six-five and the brown of his skin made his muscular physique appear to be sculpted from stone. There was no doubt in his mind that the other employees would see worse if Zeke decided to stay a while, so he might as well cut off any thoughts they may have about Zeke. "You need something?"

"Yeah, there's a guy out front, Wyatt Black. He said he worked tending bar at Fallon's on Fifth after Jigger got thrown in jail. He wants to know if we have any openings left." The entire time Holt spoke, he didn't take his eyes off the cock in Reid's hand.

Reid looked down at Zeke. "You think we'll get busy enough for two full-time bartenders?"

"If you can afford it," Zeke answered.

Reid appreciated Zeke's calm. It was nice to know Zeke was easing into the exhibitionist lifestyle that Reid preferred. He glanced back up at Holt. "Go ahead and give him a couple of T-shirts, ask him if he can start tonight and tell him that I'll be out in a few minutes."

"Will do." Holt backed out of the room. "One more question."

Reid bent down and kissed Zeke before answering. "Yeah?"

"Does this mean the employee fraternization rule is out the window?"

Reid grinned. "I already know you and Jude aren't just roommates, so yeah, I guess so."

"Thanks." Holt licked his lips before closing the door.

"Now, where were we?" Reid murmured before sealing his lips over Zeke's.

Chapter Four

Kade was tired by the time he pulled into Jace's driveway and turned off the Harley's engine. "You think they're still up?" he asked, taking off his helmet.

Lark stretched his arms over his head and yawned. "It's only eleven thirty. It just feels like it's later than that." He kissed Kade's neck. "You called and told Jace we were leaving today and not tomorrow, right?"

"Yeah." Kade took a deep breath. They hadn't planned to leave Cattle Valley until Sunday morning, but, after another night with no sleep, he'd decided not to put the meeting with Zeke off any longer.

Lark climbed off the motorcycle. "Come on."

Kade was still sitting on the bike when the front door of the house opened. He threw up his hand in greeting and got off. "Sorry we're later than we thought. Lark had a little spell, so we had to stop and get him properly fed." He pulled his backpack out of the bike's saddlebag before following Lark up the sidewalk.

Lark gave Jace a quick kiss on the cheek as he went into the house.

Jace stopped Kade at the top of the steps and hugged him. "How're you doing?"

Kade closed his eyes and sank into Jace's strong embrace. It had been years since he and Jace had been lovers, but the man still gave the best hugs. "Nervous. Excited." He squeezed Jace back before breaking contact. "I thought I might leave Lark here and ride into town."

Jace narrowed his eyes. "Why don't I drive ya?"

"Are you trying to babysit me?" Not that Kade minded. It would be nice to have some time alone with his best friend.

"Not really. I had more than enough to drink last night. This way, you can have a few if you need 'em and not worry about driving home." Jace took the backpack out of Kade's hand. "Let me grab my keys."

Kade followed Jace inside. "I need to hit the can, and tell Lark we're leaving."

After a quick hug and hello from Sam, Kade used the restroom. He'd been dying to pee for the last hour or so, so he couldn't help but groan in gratitude as he emptied his bladder. While he washed his hands, he studied his reflection in the mirror. His hair could use a good brushing before he met his brother again after twenty years, but he couldn't do a damn thing about the little lines that had begun to form around his eyes. "You're getting old," he told himself, turning away from the mirror.

Kade ran into Lark in the hallway. "You too?" he asked, assuming Lark also needed to use the restroom.

Lark wrapped his arms around Kade's waist. "Just wanted to give you a hug and kiss before you left."

"You're not mad that I'm going without you, are ya?" Kade still felt bad that he'd kept Lark somewhat at arm's length the last few days, but he didn't want his feelings about the past to interfere with his relationship.

"No." Lark pulled Kade's head down for a deep kiss before letting go. "I'll be here when you get back."

"I love you," Kade reminded Lark.

"I know." Lark turned and walked with Kade into the living room. "Sam suggested a barbecue with our friends tomorrow. Maybe you can get Zeke to come, and I can meet him there."

Kade looked at Jace, who nodded. "Depends on how tonight goes, but if it feels right I'll ask him."

"Why don't you move your bike, and I'll pull the car out of the garage?" Jace suggested after giving Sam a kiss goodbye.

"Sure." Kade grabbed the hairbrush out of his backpack before heading outside. He pushed his bike onto the sidewalk before pulling the elastic band from his hair. As Jace eased his sedan out of the garage, Kade took the time to tidy up his tangled mess of hair.

Once Kade was in the car with Jace, he held up the band. "Should I put it back again or leave it down?"

Jace chuckled. "Nervous?"

Kade wrapped the hairband around the handle of the brush and tossed it onto the floor by his feet. "Stupid, huh?"

"No." Jace reached over and squeezed Kade's shoulder. He cleared his throat. "Lark mentioned that you still haven't really talked to him about it."

"What can I say to Lark that doesn't make me sound like a complete and utter piece of shit? I abandoned my baby brother without a thought as to what it would do to him. Here it is, twenty years later, and I find out that he's been looking for me." Kade dragged his fingers through his hair. "I'm fucking ashamed of myself, man, and I don't want Lark to know the full truth of what I did."

Jace glanced at Kade before returning his attention to the road. "What'd you do? I doubt there's much that Lark wouldn't forgive you for."

"It's not about Lark forgiving me—he'd do that in a heartbeat. But I don't want him to know the man I was before..." Kade's throat seized as he tried to speak around the long-buried emotions. "Zeke's the one who caught me in the garage with an older guy who was helping me with my first motorcycle. That was about two months before my dad confronted me and asked me point blank if I was a fag. I tried to lie at first, but he kept pushing, so I finally owned up to who I was. Dad went crazy and started throwing shit and telling me I was a demon."

"And?" Jace urged Kade to continue.

"I blamed Zeke for the whole fucking thing," Kade finally admitted.

"To his face?" Jace sounded as disgusted with Kade as Kade was with himself.

"No, the only thing I said to him was something shitty like, 'See ya later, kid'." Kade took a deep breath. "I was a fucking coward. I tried to convince my dad that Zeke was lying about what he saw. Of course, the second I saw the confusion on Dad's face, I knew that Zeke hadn't said anything, but I'd already planted the seed in my dad's head. No telling what he did to Zeke after I left."

Jace was silent for several minutes. He turned into the club parking lot and switched off the engine. "I guess now I know why you didn't jump at the chance to see Zeke again."

"Yeah." Kade's stomach clenched at the thought of going inside the bar. "I don't even know why he's been looking for me. Is it because he's missed me or is he planning to shoot my ass?"

"Probably the first, but in case it's the second, don't worry."

"You gonna protect me?" Kade asked.

"Nope. I'm going to convince him that a few hard hits to your face should do the trick, and I'll hold your arms behind your back while he does it." Jace jiggled the keys in his hand. "I love you, and that'll never change, but he deserves some retribution if that's what he's after."

"I know, and you won't need to hold my arms. I'd let him beat the shit out of me if I thought it would make things all right between us."

"Then let's go," Jace said, opening the car door.

* * * *

Zeke handed Wyatt another bottle of Jack Daniel's. "Watch out for that guy on the end, I had trouble with him last night."

Wyatt nodded. "He's already propositioned me twice."

"Yeah, well, if he gives you any more trouble, tell Jude or Holt." Zeke went back to filling orders. He felt eyes on him and glanced up to see Reid staring at him from the hallway. Zeke crooked his finger, beckoning the man he couldn't get enough of.

Reid was on his way over, when something caught his attention. He turned and stared at the two men sitting a few tables away before glancing back at Zeke with worry in his expression.

Zeke looked at the men. He recognized the one on the left from the previous night. His heart stopped when his gaze landed on the man to his right. Taking a step back, Zeke reached blindly for something to steady himself on. Unwanted tears quickly filled his eyes as he fought like hell to keep his composure.

Reid was there in an instant to wrap Zeke in his arms. "It's okay," Reid whispered in Zeke's ear as Zeke clung to him. "Let me take you to the office. The two of you can meet in there."

Zeke pulled back and stared up at Reid. "Did you know he was coming tonight?"

"No." Reid gave Zeke a tender kiss. "If you want me to tell him to leave, I will."

Zeke shook his head and again tried to steady himself. Once more he looked toward the table and felt panic well up inside him when he found Kade's chair empty. Scanning the crowd, he searched for his brother. "Where'd he go?"

"He headed to the bathroom when he saw that he'd upset you," Reid explained.

Zeke squared his shoulders. "I'm gonna go talk to him."

"Take him into the office," Reid suggested.

"Sure, if things get that far."

Zeke started to head to the restroom, but Reid pulled him back. "*Make* things get that far. You've searched too long to let this chance slip through your fingers."

The emotion in Reid's expression surprised Zeke. They'd only known each other for a few days and already Reid's genuine concern was more than he'd ever had or expected from a lover. "Okay. I'm going now before I chicken out."

Reid gave a gentle smile and kissed Zeke again. "I'll be out here helping Wyatt if you need me."

"Thanks." Zeke broke away and pushed his way through the crowd toward the back hallway. The men's room was the second door on the left and once he reached it, he stopped. "This is the moment you've been waiting for," he whispered to himself.

Zeke took several deep breaths before opening the door.

Kade spun around like he was looking for a fight, but his expression softened in a single breath. "Hey."

Zeke stared at his brother and suddenly he was eight years old again. "I didn't do it. I didn't tell Dad," he blurted out.

"I know," Kade said in a voice so soft Zeke barely heard him.

Zeke took a step back and turned toward the door. "I've spent ten years of my fucking life searching the country to tell you that, and you already know!" he screamed. Another thought struck him. "You never tried to get in touch with me. I thought you really blamed me for what Dad did, but that wasn't it at all. You didn't love me." He reached for the door handle.

Kade's hand slammed against the door, keeping it shut. "Don't walk away like I did." His hand curled into a fist. "I've hated myself for years for what I did to you."

Zeke pressed his heated face against the cool metal of the door. "So why didn't you do something about it?"

"Because I was an eighteen-year-old asshole when I left, and by the time life caught up with me, years had gone by. I didn't figure you'd want anything to do with me. Hell, I barely wanted anything to do with me. I was a messed-up, depressed motherfucker that used other men to try to kill myself."

"What's that supposed to mean?" Zeke mumbled. He refused to feel sorry for Kade.

"I'm HIV positive," Kade said. He released the door. "If you want to leave, I won't stop you. If you want to rip my head off, I won't stop you from doing that either. But I need you to know that I love you, and if I could change only one thing that's happened in my life, it would be the way I left you."

HIV positive. What would Zeke have done if Kade had died before he'd had a chance to find him? He knew he couldn't let his anger drive them apart again. "Reid said we could use his office if we wanted to sit down and talk." He glanced over his shoulder. "That's where I'm going now. If you want to follow me that would be great."

* * * *

Jace joined Reid at the bar after last call. "They've been in there a long time."

Reid nodded. It had taken everything he had not to check on Zeke, but he knew it was something the two brothers needed to work out on their own. "Tell me more about Kade."

"He's my best friend," Jace replied. "I've known him for years, but there's always been a part of himself that he refused to share. He'd sink into these God-awful bouts of depression for months at a time. I guess now I know why."

Reid wanted to hate Kade for what he'd done to Zeke, but he couldn't. Henry, Reid's oldest brother, had suffered periods of depression, so he knew first-hand how the illness could affect someone's ability to make the right decisions. "What else can you tell me?"

Jace shook his head. "If you want to know what kind of man Kade is, you'll need to talk to him yourself. Correct me if I'm wrong, but you've already become protective of Zeke, and nothing I say is going to convince you that Kade's a good man unless you figure it out on your own."

Reid couldn't refute what Jace had said, so he didn't try.

Jace took a cocktail napkin off the pile in front of Reid and wrote an address on it. "Sammy and I are having a get-together tomorrow with Kade, Lark and our other friends from town. Alec and Max should be there, if that makes you more comfortable. Bring Zeke and find out for yourself what Kade is like."

Reid stared at the address. "It's up to Zeke, but if he's interested we'll be there."

When Kade walked back into the room, he looked like he'd been through hell. He stopped beside Jace and pounded him on the back. "I'm ready." He looked at Reid. "Zeke's asking for you."

"How'd it go?" Reid asked.

"Well, we talked for over three hours and he didn't hit me, so I suppose we're on the road," Kade answered.

Reid went over to speak to Wyatt. "Can you handle closing?"

Wyatt nodded. "Want me to balance out the register?"

"Yeah. Just drop the bag by my office on your way out." Reid knocked his knuckles against the bar as he passed Jace and Kade. "I'll call you in the morning once I find out what Zeke wants to do."

"Sure thing," Jace said, climbing off the bar stool.

Reid watched as Jace wrapped an arm around Kade and led him out of the bar. He turned and went to his office. "Zeke," he said as he pushed open the door.

Zeke was sitting in Reid's large leather desk chair. "Is he gone?"

"Yeah." Reid bent and picked Zeke up before sitting in his chair. He settled Zeke on his lap. "I have to say, Kade looked worse than you do."

Zeke leaned against Reid's chest. "He should. I had to be the one to tell him that both our parents are dead." He started to unbutton Reid's white dress shirt. "I'm not going to lie, it was hard, but we managed to share a few funny stories by the time he left."

Reid untucked his shirt. "So the two of you are good?" He wasn't sure how Zeke could be horny after the night he'd had, but Reid would sure as hell give the man anything he wanted.

Zeke pulled his tight T-shirt off over his head before settling against Reid's bare chest.

When Zeke reached for the fly of Reid's jeans, Reid stopped him. "Are you sure you feel like doing this?"

"Uh-huh," Zeke said. "I've had enough of feeling bad for one night. I need you to help me feel good."

Reid tilted Zeke's chin up and gave him a deep kiss. "Take your clothes off."

Zeke stood and quickly undressed while Reid pushed his jeans down to his ankles. "You brought stuff down, right?" Zeke asked, straddling Reid's lap.

Reid opened his top right drawer and removed a bottle of lube. He accepted Zeke's kiss as he poured a good amount of the slick stuff onto his finger. "Nice," he whispered when Zeke pulled back.

"Fuck me." Zeke ran his tongue up the side of Reid's face.

Within seconds, Reid had a condom rolled down the length of his erection. He slathered Zeke's hole with lube before holding his cock by the base. "I'm all yours. Take it."

Zeke eased down onto Reid's cock as they both moaned. "So big," Zeke groaned.

The door opened without warning and Alec stepped inside. "Fuck."

"Shit." Reid reached for his discarded dress shirt and covered Zeke's ass. "What the hell're you doing here at this time of night?"

Alec didn't look the least bit embarrassed at the situation, but why should he? Alec had watched Reid fuck a ton of guys when they had been roommates. "Jace called and said it might be nice of me to come by and help you close up tonight." He took the chair in front of Reid's desk and laid the money out. "You have an adding machine?"

Reid nodded toward the device in front of him. "If it was a snake, it'd have bit ya."

Zeke moaned softly in Reid's ear as he started to move. "Can't hold still," he whispered.

Reid made sure Zeke's ass was covered as Zeke slowly moved his hips back and forth. It wasn't an all-out fucking, but it was enough to turn Reid on. "How's it looking?" he asked, turning his attention to the pile of cash and charge slips.

"Pretty good from this side of the desk," Alec replied, his gaze on Zeke.

"I meant tonight's take." With the desire to touch Zeke's bare skin becoming too strong, Reid gave up holding the shirt and simply tied the sleeves around Zeke's waist. His hands free, he pushed them under the shirt and grabbed Zeke's ass.

Zeke gave Reid another deep kiss while Alec answered, "I don't know yet. I can't seem to concentrate."

Zeke broke the kiss and glanced over his shoulder. "You like to watch?"

"From time to time," Alec answered. "Although I can guarantee if Max was here, we sure as hell wouldn't be watching the two of you."

"What would you be doing instead?" Zeke asked.

Reid peppered kisses on the nape of Zeke's neck. It was obvious that Zeke was enjoying himself. Was it possible he'd finally met his match in a partner?"

"Same thing you're doing, I'd imagine." Alec chuckled. "Watching Reid show off has always made me horny."

"He has a nice cock, doesn't he?" Zeke asked. He reached out and pushed against the desk until the chair spun to the side, making it easier for him to look at Alec.

"I've never messed with Reid, if that's what you're asking," Alec fired back.

"It wasn't." Zeke ground his ass against Reid. "So why don't you call Max?"

"Because it's past his bedtime." Alec narrowed his eyes. "What kind of ideas are in that pretty head of yours?"

Zeke shrugged. "I'm new to fucking in front of other people — guess I'm trying to figure out how far I'm willing to go with it."

Reid thrust up hard, driving his cock deeper into Zeke's ass. He stared at his best friend. "I think I've died and gone to heaven."

Alec broke eye contact with Zeke to glance at Reid. Unspoken dialog bounced between them, and Reid knew that Alec was well aware of what Zeke meant to him. "Why don't you go home to Max, and I'll take care of the receipts before I go upstairs."

Alec nodded. "Yeah, I think I will." He stood and smiled at Reid. "Will I see you both tomorrow?"

Reid realized he hadn't talked to Zeke about the gathering at Jace's. *Shit.*

Zeke spoke first. "I haven't asked Reid yet, but I'm hoping we'll be able to go."

Reid squeezed Zeke's ass. He was moments away from fucking him for real. "See you tomorrow, Alec."

Alec took the hint. "'Night."

The moment Alec was out of the door, Reid wrapped his arms around Zeke and stood with his cock still buried. He laid Zeke on the desk and couldn't believe the picture the younger man made. Zeke's lips were parted as Reid fucked him hard. "You liked having Alec watch us, didn't you?"

"Yeah," Zeke said. "I didn't think I would, but it was a rush to know he wanted to be you."

Not even Alec could deny the truth in Zeke's statement, but he couldn't let it just sit there without taking a jab at Zeke. "Or maybe he wanted to be you," he said, giving Zeke something to think about. He draped Zeke's legs over his shoulders and leaned down to kiss him. "But I wouldn't begrudge Alec the thought of being in my position right now."

Zeke grinned. "And I wouldn't begrudge him for being in mine."

* * * *

After a quiet ride home, Kade walked into Jace's house and immediately went to his old room, bypassing Lark and Sammy without saying a word. He knew Lark would be in any second to check on him.

Right on time, Lark walked into the room. "You okay?"

Kade stepped out of his jeans and turned his back on Lark while he pulled back the covers. "I'm better than I should be—better than I have a right to be." He sat on the edge of the bed and waited for Lark to get undressed. "Did you have a nice evening with Sammy?"

"Sure. We always have fun together, but I was worried about you." Lark grabbed his backpack and took out a small toiletry bag.

Kade expected Lark to set lube and condoms on the bedside table. When Lark pulled out his toothbrush and toothpaste and stuffed the rest back into his pack, Kade felt a sinking in his gut. "Have you given up on me?"

Lark paused on the way to the adjoining bathroom. "What did you say?"

"Nothing," Kade mumbled.

"I've been tiptoeing around you for days, what more do you want from me?" Lark asked.

Kade had fucked up and he knew it. "The problem isn't what I want from you. It's what you deserve from me that you haven't been getting lately."

Lark disappeared into the bathroom without saying a word.

Kade slid under the covers and turned out the bedside lamp. He thought of Zeke and what he must have gone through when Kade had left home. Lark would come out of the bathroom any moment, and Kade knew it, but the act of his beloved walking away had cut him to the bone. How had an eight-year-old survived it?

Lark turned off the bathroom light before opening the door. His lean body was silhouetted perfectly by the moonlight that streamed through the windows as he made his way around the end of the bed to the opposite side. Once under the covers, Lark scooted to Kade and rested his head on Kade's chest like he did every night. "For the record, I'm not some nymphomaniac who has to be fucked every night to be kept happy. I'm not stupid, Kade, I know you're dealing with a lot of shit right now that doesn't involve me. I'd be lying if I said it didn't hurt that you're shutting me out, but I *understand*."

Kade wrapped his arms around Lark and hugged him. What could he possibly say? "A year after I left town, my dad killed himself. He actually took the time to clean out the garage so he could park his car inside. When Zeke came home from school, he noticed all the bicycles and shit in the driveway. He opened the garage door and found my father dead inside his Buick, the engine still running." He made a disgusted sound. "Mom had been constantly on his back for running me off, and evidently he felt he couldn't take it anymore." He growled. "Who the fuck knows why that sorry son of a bitch did what he did, but why did it have to be Zeke who found him?"

"I'm sorry," Lark said. He turned his head and gave Kade's chest a soft kiss.

"Don't be sorry for me. Zeke's the one who grew up without a father." Kade swallowed around the lump in his throat. "Mom died of a heart attack when Zeke was seventeen." He shook his head. "Isaiah was forced to come home from college to take care of Zeke until he graduated high school, and, according to Zeke, Isaiah still hasn't forgiven him for it."

"Zeke's still in contact with your other brother?" Lark asked.

"Yeah, kinda. He knows where Isaiah lives at least. I guess they only talk a couple times a year, though."

"So will you call him?"

Kade ran his palm up and down Lark's back. "Probably. Zeke and I have agreed to try to work things out. Maybe Isaiah'll be next."

"Sounds like a pretty good plan to me."

Kade closed his eyes. Lark had been right—he'd done absolutely everything a supportive partner should do, and still Kade had kept him in the dark. "Zeke will be at the barbecue tomorrow, and I'd like it if you'd try to get to know him."

"Sure. You don't even need to ask." Lark scooted up and kissed Kade. "If someone's important to you, they're important to me."

"Yeah, well, I think I need to fill you in on the whole story before you meet him." Kade prayed Lark would understand, but he knew, whether Lark approved of what he'd done or not, his boyfriend wouldn't stop loving him.

Chapter Five

"Should I tuck this in?" Zeke asked. His nerves were frazzled and the fact that he didn't have anything appropriate to wear for a barbecue should've been the last thing on his mind. Unfortunately, he only had four changes of clothes and all of them were bartender appropriate, not meeting-your-brother's-partner-and-friends appropriate.

Reid stepped up behind him. "You look great." He wrapped his arms around Zeke and pushed his hand up under the tight T-shirt.

Zeke leaned back against Reid's broad chest and studied the two of them in the mirror. "If you weren't so damn big, I'd steal something from your closet."

Reid rubbed Zeke's chest. "If I had my way, I think I'd rather have you shirtless with those short cut-offs you pulled out of your bag earlier."

"I can't wear those around you. At least not in public." Zeke tilted his head to the side as Reid kissed it.

"Afraid I won't be able to keep my hands off of you?" Reid nipped the skin under Zeke's ear.

"They're too low and short for a hard-on, unless I want to get arrested." Zeke ran a hand over his hair. He was due for another buzz cut, but it could wait. With his hands shaking the way they were, he'd end up making a mess. "Do you know how to use hair clippers?"

"Sure." Reid moved to cup Zeke's cock. "You need a trim, babe?"

Although most of Zeke's groin had been waxed to accommodate his low-rise jeans, he did have a small patch of hair just above his cock. "Tell you what, when we get home you can take the clippers to every inch of hair on my body. How's that?"

"Sounds perfect." Reid released Zeke and took a step back. "We're going to miss the food if we don't get going."

"You'll have to drive. My Harley only has room for one." Zeke turned around to face Reid. "This is almost like a real date."

"It is a real date," Reid corrected. "And I hope to be compensated accordingly at the end of the evening."

Zeke agreed wholeheartedly. He couldn't seem to get enough of Reid's cock, and, even better, he actually enjoyed his time with Reid between bouts of fucking. It was rare for him, almost unheard of, in fact. "And I shall willingly pay that bill with my body and mouth."

* * * *

"This is huge!" Zeke said, getting into Reid's white Escalade. "You could fuck in an SUV like this."

"Alec told me to buy something that was heavy enough to get around in the snow." Reid liked the SUV okay, but he preferred the Jaguar he'd owned in

Philadelphia. "And, for the record, you can fuck in a Volkswagen Beetle if you want to bad enough."

"True," Zeke agreed. He stared out of the side window for several moments. "So what's the story with Alec and Max? Why'd he say it was after Max's bedtime?"

"They live a D/s lifestyle, and Alec has Max on a fairly strict schedule," Reid explained.

"I don't get that. Why would a grown man let another man treat him that way?"

"I don't know the whole story, but evidently Max does much better on a structured schedule. I guess he had some issues with depression and stuff before Alec came along." Reid shrugged. "All I know is that I've never seen Alec happier, and, from what Jace has told me, Max is the same way." He stopped at a light and turned to Zeke. "I've learnt not to question other couples' lifestyle choices because most of them don't agree with mine."

"Yeah, you're right. It just seemed weird to me."

Reid released Zeke's hand and moved to cup his cock. "And me doing this in hopes of a semi driving by is weird to a lot of other people."

"Touché." Zeke chuckled. "By the way, if you want people to watch you jack me off, you should've gotten a shorter vehicle."

"I bought it before you came to town." Reid continued to massage Zeke's cock through the denim. "But, if I can convince you to stick around for a while, I'll lease a low-slung convertible for the warmer weather."

"Interesting proposal, but I'm not sure what my plans are yet. I guess it depends on how well things go today with Kade and his partner."

Reid had half expected the answer, but it still cut deep. "If it helps you make up your mind or anything, I'd like you to stay."

* * * *

Zeke climbed out of the SUV and grabbed the sack of chips and dip from the back seat while Reid retrieved the cooler full of pop and beer. He felt somewhat shitty for not commenting on Reid's desire for him to stick around. If he truly had reached the end of the line in looking for Kade, things might've been different, but that wasn't the case.

"Ya coming?" Reid asked as he started toward the backyard.

"Yeah." Zeke caught up with Reid. He'd figure stuff out with Reid later. Now, he had an entire group of strangers to meet. *I can do this*, he told himself. He was a bartender, after all, he was used to talking to people he didn't know.

Reid set the cooler down and opened the privacy gate. Before Zeke went through, Reid stopped him. "Just relax and let it happen." He gave Zeke a deep kiss. "And if at any time you're ready to leave, just say the word."

"Thanks." Zeke led the way. *I can do this*, he repeated to himself. He had a strong feeling it would be his mantra for the day. There had to be at least twenty men in the backyard, and he didn't recognize any of them. "Who're all these people?"

"I'll introduce you to the ones I know, but you're on your own with the rest." Reid chuckled. He set the cooler down with the others. "You want something?"

"Just a water for now." Zeke felt like everyone was staring at him. Awkward. "You see Kade?"

Reid handed Zeke a bottle. "I see him. He's headed our way."

Kade came toward them with a much younger, much smaller man in tow. "Hey." He gave Zeke a hug. "Glad you came."

Zeke closed his eyes as he fully accepted the embrace. He was glad the two of them had taken the time the night before to work through the initial awkwardness.

"I love you," Kade whispered in Zeke's ear.

"I swear to God, if you make me cry in front of all these people, I'm gonna kill you." Zeke stepped back and stared up at his big brother. "I just want you to know, you were worth the search."

Kade's eyes filled with tears. "You fucker." He grabbed Zeke and put him into a headlock.

Zeke squirmed and stomped on Kade's heavy biker boot. It was the same shit Kade used to pull when they were younger except, back then, Zeke hadn't been big enough to fight back. Not that he was honestly fighting his brother, but he had to at least hold his own.

"Kade, knock it off," someone said.

Kade let go, and Zeke rubbed his burning ears.

"Did I hurt you?" Kade asked.

"In your dreams." Zeke grinned. Although they were just playing, it was more than he could've hoped for. He decided to reach out to Kade's partner. "You must be my big brother's tamer, Lark."

"Something like that." Lark ignored Zeke's outstretched hand and hugged him instead. "It's nice to meet you."

Zeke broke their embrace and gestured to Reid. "This is Reid." He wasn't sure what to call Reid. *My boss? My lover?* "A good friend of mine," he eventually settled on.

"You own Clean Slate with Alec, right?" Lark asked.

"Yes. Alec and I have been friends since college." Reid shook Lark's hand.

"Come on, I'll introduce you to a few of my friends." Kade slung his arm around Zeke's neck and led him away from Reid and Lark. "How serious is it with you and Reid?"

Zeke wasn't sure how to answer. Reid was such a new addition to his life that he knew it would sound weird to go on and on about how much he liked the guy, but he couldn't deny how Reid made him feel. "I like him. It's hard to explain, but there's something about him that makes me feel grounded. Believe me, for someone who's moved around as much as I have, that's a pretty big thing."

Kade shook his head. "You don't have to convince me. Lark saved my life. When I met him, I was in the midst of full-on depression." He grinned. "Lark wasn't having it. He threatened to kick my ass if I didn't snap out of it."

Zeke tried to imagine someone of Lark's stature threatening his big brother. "He must've really cared for you."

"Yeah, and I still haven't figured out why. Just like I can't believe you cared enough to search all this time for me. I've never believed I was worth either of those things." Kade rubbed the top of Zeke's head before kissing it. "I feel better at this moment than I have since I left home. Thanks for not giving up on me."

* * * *

Relaxing in a lawn chair under the biggest tree in the yard, Reid watched as Kade and Zeke talked to a group that had gathered around them. "Kade hasn't let Zeke out of his sight."

"Can't say that I blame him," Alec replied.

Neither could Reid, but it bothered him on a purely selfish level. The closer the two brothers became, the less chance Reid had of convincing Zeke to stay. "Do you think he'll go back to Cattle Valley with Kade?"

"Probably, but you had to know that when you fucked him the first time, right?" Alec opened the cooler beside him and withdrew another water.

"I didn't really think about it at the time because I'm not used to getting attached." Reid couldn't take his eyes off Zeke. Christ, he was completely and utterly obsessed.

"But you're already at that point," Alec surmised.

"Yeah, I am. I fucked my way through Philadelphia without an inkling of what I feel now." Reid thought of all the men he'd walked away from after a long weekend of fucking and knew Zeke didn't belong in that category.

"You need to give him some room. His world changed in a matter of days. If you pressure him, he may crack."

Reid rolled his eyes. "Words of wisdom from the big Greek."

Max broke away from a conversation with Sam to join Alec and Reid. He settled on the grass between Alec's legs and leaned back. "So, what're the antisocial twins up to over here?"

Alec leaned forwards and down to whisper something in Max's ear. Reid wasn't sure what was said, but Max blushed and nodded. Alec sat back in his chair and began to play with Max's hair.

Max looked up at Reid. "Zeke's great. He seems really comfortable around everyone."

Reid returned his attention to Zeke. "Maybe he'll make some friends here."

"Probably, but I heard him tell Rocco that he was thinking of giving Cattle Valley a try," Max said. He received a slight slap to the top of his head from Alec. Max looked up at Alec, obviously confused. Alec met Max's gaze and the two seemed to do that mental conversation thing that Reid had seen before.

The last thing Reid wanted was for Max to start backtracking on what he'd let slip. "I think I'll find a bathroom." He headed toward the house before Max and Alec could finish their mental argument.

Reid found Jace in the kitchen talking to several men. "I didn't know the party was in here, too," he said, announcing his presence.

Jace smiled. "Hey, Reid. You remember Tony and his partner Daniel?"

"Sure." Reid shook hands with both men.

"And I don't think you've met Joe Pressman," Jace introduced.

Reid shook hands with the distinguished-looking man. "Nice to meet you."

"And you." Joe gestured to the French doors leading outside. "Have you met my partner Rocco?"

"Not yet." The mention of Rocco's name reminded Reid why he'd come into the house in the first place.

"I was just telling Tony how well the club opening went the other night," Jace said.

"Thanks. We weren't sure how people would embrace the club after what happened there before, but we had another good crowd last night." Reid leaned back against the counter and crossed his arms.

The door opened and Zeke walked into the kitchen. He crooked a finger at Reid. "Excuse me, but can I talk to you for a minute?"

"Sure." Reid broke away from the other men. He followed Zeke down the hall and into the bathroom. "What's going on?"

"I started to panic when I looked up and you weren't sitting next to Alec. I went over and asked where you were, and Max told me what he'd said." Zeke started to unzip his jeans. "Sorry, I have to pee so bad I wasn't sure I could make it."

"Me too." It said a lot about how comfortable Reid was when he stepped up beside Zeke at the toilet. Zeke grinned and reached over to hold Reid's cock while he relieved himself. Sexy was the word that came to mind.

"I like the way you let me touch you whenever I want," Zeke said.

Reid's cock started to harden, which didn't make it easy to pee. "If I had my way, you'd want to touch me every minute of the day," he replied in all honesty.

"Who said I don't? But I don't think there's anyone here, other than maybe Alec and Max, who cares to see me walking around with my hands down your pants."

Reid was finally able to empty his bladder. Thank the heavens. "It's a little hard to have your hands down my pants from across the yard." As soon as he said the words, he wished he could take them back. *Fuck. I sound like a needy bitch.* "Never mind, forget I said that."

Zeke released Reid's cock and zipped his jeans. "I'm just trying to figure shit out right now."

"I know, which is why I shouldn't have said anything." Reid went to the sink and turned on the water. "It's nice to see you having a good time."

"I am." Zeke squirted liquid soap into his hands and rubbed them together before reaching for Reid's. He entwined their fingers and suddenly washing their hands became so much more. "Today's for Kade, but tonight's for us."

Reid nodded. He wanted a night, but he needed more of them. "So you've decided to go to Cattle Valley?"

Zeke pushed their hands under the water to wash the soap off. "Yeah, I think so. At least until I figure out what's next."

Reid grabbed a hand towel off the edge of the sink and dried his hands before passing it to Zeke. There wasn't much else to say at that point. Reid had little choice but to deal with Zeke's decision. It wasn't that he didn't understand Zeke's desire to get closer to his brother, but Kade already had a life that he loved. Reid wished he was confident enough to say something to Zeke, but it had only been a few days, what right did he have?

"We'd better get out of here in case someone else needs to go." Reid took the towel from Zeke and hung it up. He quickly checked his appearance in the mirror before opening the door.

"You're mad, huh?"

"I'm not mad, there's just not a lot I can say at this point." Reid was honest, he wasn't mad. Jealous, maybe, and a teensy bit heartbroken, but he definitely wasn't mad. He knew he had two choices—he could walk away now or treat Zeke like he did all the lovers that had come before him. Unfortunately, he wasn't sure if he could live with either option. *Fuck.*

Reid left Zeke standing in his dust as he hotfooted it out of the bathroom. *What the hell?* Zeke took off toward the kitchen only to see Reid pass by Jace and the others without saying a word. *Damn, I'm glad he's not mad.*

Zeke plastered on a smile as he made his way into the kitchen. "Great party. Thanks for having it," he told Jace.

"You're welcome. I'm glad things seem to be going well for you and Kade," Jace replied.

"Yeah, they are." Zeke excused himself and stepped outside. Reid was back in his chair beside Alec, but, instead of the water he'd been drinking all day, Reid had a beer in his hand. When Reid caught Zeke looking at him, he quickly turned his head away and started talking to Alec.

Frustrated, Zeke sighed. He moved to stand by Kade. "Mind if I have one of your beers?"

"Not at all." Kade fished a bottle out of the melting ice and handed it to Zeke. "Everything okay?"

Zeke had never been in the position to ask his big brother for advice, but he sure as hell didn't want to start when he was surrounded by other people. He glanced at Reid again. Earlier in the day, Reid had seemed to watch his every move. Now, Reid couldn't seem to care less. "Can we go for a walk?"

"Sure. Just let me tell Lark." Kade crossed over to where Lark was stretched out on a blanket talking to Sam, Rocco and Michael. He leaned down and gave Lark a kiss before jogging back over. "Did you talk to Reid?"

Zeke shook his head. "I doubt that he cares at the moment, but I'll mention it to him."

Kade pulled two more beers from the cooler and passed another to Zeke as they headed toward Reid. "Meet you at the gate."

Once he was closer to Reid, Zeke noticed the sadness in the man's big brown eyes. "I'm gonna go for a quick walk with Kade, but I'll be back before you miss me."

Reid nodded. "I need to be out of here by five so I can work on the books."

"Okay." Before Zeke walked off, he pressed his palm against Reid's cheek, hoping for some sign that he hadn't lost the man completely.

Although Reid made no move to reciprocate the gesture, Zeke did feel a slight pressure against his palm as if Reid wanted to lean into the touch but couldn't commit. Zeke wasn't an idiot, he knew why Reid was suddenly giving him the cold shoulder. He simply wished they'd waited to discuss it. His feelings toward Reid hadn't changed despite their current predicament. He placed a soft, but quick kiss on Reid's temple. "We won't be long."

Zeke joined Kade at the gate and they headed north down the tree-lined street. "It really is a pretty town," Zeke commented as they passed a row of renovated Victorian houses.

"It's a great place to live," Kade agreed. He pointed out an area of the sidewalk where the roots of a giant tree had buckled the pavement. "Careful, there's a hazard up ahead."

"So why'd you move to Cattle Valley?" Zeke stopped in front of a pale yellow clapboard bungalow with a profusion of flowers up the walk and pouring out of window boxes. He completely zoned out as he stared. It might have been the first time since he'd left home that he longed to live in a house.

"It's pretty," Kade said from beside him.

The house was more than just a pretty building to Zeke. He'd been a vagabond for so long he had no idea what it would feel like to build an actual life for himself. What would it be like to make friends knowing you could keep them? "Yeah," he agreed. He turned away from the house and started back down the sidewalk.

"So what happened between you and Reid?" Kade asked after several blocks of silence.

"I told him I was planning to go back to Cattle Valley with you for a while. At least until I figure out what the hell I'm supposed to do now." Zeke handed Kade back the beer that he was no longer in the mood for.

"What you're supposed to do is live your own life for a change."

"I hear ya. The problem is that I'm not sure how to do that. As long as I had you to search for, I had a reason to get up in the morning. Now what?" The only thing Zeke was trained to do was to be a bartender, and he wasn't sure he wanted to do that for the rest of his life. "When do you think you'll head back to Wyoming?"

Kade looked up and down the street before quickly depositing the beer bottles in a nearby trash can that someone had left at the end of their driveway. "I'm not sure. I'll talk to Lark and let you know."

Zeke couldn't believe Kade had done that. He opened the trash can and dug the bottles out. "You're not supposed to throw glass in the garbage. Jeez, don't they recycle where you come from?"

"Sure they do, but usually I just have to set the bottles and cans in the sink and Lark takes care of it."

Kade shrugged. "I didn't feel like carrying them back to Jace's.

"Fine. I'll do it." Zeke cradled the three bottles in one arm. "So what do you think I should do about Reid?" Zeke asked.

"Sorry, I don't think I can answer that for you. I have my opinions, but the only one that really counts is yours."

"I like Reid a lot, but I've been searching for you for so long that it'd be stupid not to move to where I can get to know you again." Zeke looked up at the sky. "What time is it?"

Kade pulled out his cellphone. "Four thirty-five. Wanna head back?"

"Yeah." Zeke turned and walked back toward Jace's neighborhood.

"Are you planning to go home with Reid?"

Zeke nodded, but didn't offer an explanation as to why. Quite frankly, he wasn't sure himself. It was obvious that Reid wasn't thrilled with him at the moment, but Zeke couldn't stand the thought of leaving town without making amends with someone who had begun to mean something to him.

* * * *

Reid slapped Alec's forearm. "Well, bud, I'm gonna take off."

"Don't you leave without Zeke," Alec growled.

"I told him I was leaving at five and it's two minutes 'til. Evidently he's changed his mind about going home with me." Reid got to his feet. "Sorry I've been lax on the books, but I plan to get everything caught up tonight."

"Don't worry about the damn books."

Reid picked up the cooler and headed out. He knew he should thank Jace for a good day, but he wasn't in the mood to lie to the man. Before he reached the gate, Kade and a bare-chested Zeke stepped into the backyard. It took Reid a moment, but his gaze eventually landed on the bloody T-shirt wrapped around Zeke's hand. Dropping the cooler, Reid raced over. "What happened?"

"Tripped on a damn buckle in the sidewalk and cut myself on a beer bottle," Zeke explained.

"It needs to be stitched up," Kade informed Reid. "I didn't want to mess with it too much for obvious reasons, but, from what I could see, it looks pretty bad."

Reid dug his keys out of his pocket. "Let's go."

"Don't forget the cooler," Zeke reminded Reid.

"That's the least of my concerns."

"I'm fine. I don't plan to bleed to death in the time it'll take you to load a cooler into the Escalade."

Reid retrieved the cooler, and Kade opened the gate for him. "I need to talk to Lark, but don't leave without me because I'm coming with you," Kade informed them.

Reid fought the urge to hand Kade the keys and tell him to take care of it himself. How big of an ass was he for being jealous of Zeke's renewed relationship with Kade? *Fuck.* He hoisted the cooler into the SUV before climbing into the driver's seat. As soon as Zeke was in the passenger seat, Reid reached across him and fastened his seatbelt. "You doing okay?"

Zeke shook his head. "I didn't mean to hurt your feelings earlier."

Reid brushed the apology away. "Let's just get you to the hospital."

"I don't think it's as bad as Kade does. It probably needs a few stitches, but it's just a cut."

The back door opened and Kade jumped in. "Sorry about that."

"No problem," Reid replied, trying his best to understand Kade's request to accompany them.

It was a short, quiet ride to the hospital, and by the time Reid pulled up to the Emergency Room doors he was about to go out of his mind. The closeness he'd felt with Zeke over the last few days was gone. It felt like a wall had been erected between them in the span of ninety minutes. "I'll let you off here and find a place to park."

Kade got out and opened the front passenger door. Zeke surprised Reid by leaning over the console and giving him a soft kiss. "Wish me luck. I hate needles," Zeke whispered.

"I'll be in the waiting room if you need me," Reid said, feeling a little lighter. He waited until Zeke had disappeared through the sliding glass doors before pulling out. It wasn't hard to find a place to park — evidently flu season was officially over.

Reid was inside within five minutes. "He already go back?"

Kade glanced up from the clipboard he seemed to be concentrating on. "Yeah, he was starting to feel lightheaded, so they took him on back and asked me to fill out these papers." He tapped the form with the tip of his pen. "I'm not sure what to put down for his address."

"He rents one of those by-the-week hotel rooms over on Douglas Avenue, but I don't think that's the kind of address the billing department is looking for. Just put mine down."

Kade handed Reid the clipboard. "He doesn't have any insurance, so they'll probably make him pay upfront."

Reid doubted Zeke had the money. "I'll just put my payment information down, and he can pay me back when he gets it."

"You don't have to do that. He's my brother. I can take care of it."

Reid finished filling in his credit card number and handed the clipboard back. "Already done."

Kade shook his head and returned to the form. "You don't like me much, do you?"

"I don't know you enough to answer that one way or the other." Reid decided to level with the guy. "I'm glad that Zeke found you, but I think we were really starting to build something between us. Now that you're here, Zeke can't seem to be bothered with me anymore, and, yeah, it hurts."

"For the record, I think he's feeling pretty torn right now. He really likes you, but you have to remember he's spent his entire adult life looking for me. Now that we've reconnected, he doesn't want to lose that again, and I think he's kind of drifting right now as to what to do next."

"But if he goes home with you, the last few days will have meant nothing more than a brief affair. That's not enough for me." Reid noticed that Kade had stopped filling out the form when it came to medical history.

"The two of you can still see each other. Lark and I come down every few months or so."

Reid nodded. "It's a lot easier to see a family member every few months than it is to see your boyfriend," he reminded Kade.

"Reid Jackson?" a woman at the desk called.

"That's me." Reid stood up and approached the desk.

"You're wanted in room four," she said.

"Thanks." Reid felt like kicking up his heels when he was buzzed through the security door. Zeke had asked for him, not Kade. He hated to make it sound like a competition, but in a way it was. He found Zeke stretched out on a narrow bed. "Hey."

"I thought I'd take you up on that offer." Zeke smiled. "By the way, the doctor has absolutely no sense of humor, so don't even try to amuse him."

"I'll remember that." Reid stood at Zeke's bedside. He longed to bend down and kiss Zeke, but wasn't sure where things stood with them. "Did the doctor say how many stitches?"

Zeke shook his head. "I don't think so. As soon as he mentioned numbing the wound, I mentally checked out."

Reid gave in to his desire and bent to brush a kiss across Zeke's lips. "Thanks for asking me back here."

"Don't thank me. You've given me more in a few days than I've ever had, and I'm sorry our wires got crossed earlier. I'm torn right now, and I've never been the poster child for making the best decisions. Hell, I left home with a motorcycle, a backpack and a hundred and ten bucks in my wallet. Not exactly the smartest thing I've ever done, and I'm sure I'll make a hundred more mistakes before I die."

"Let's just see how things go until you leave," Reid suggested.

The doctor came back into the exam room with a tray. Ouch. Reid wanted to be strong for Zeke but he wasn't crazy about needles either. He moved the chair from the corner of the room to the side of the bed by Zeke's head then put his back to the doctor and the bleeding cut. "Concentrate on me while he gets you sewn up."

"I can do that." Zeke winced and bit his lip. "Shot," he said between clenched jaws.

"See? You didn't scream or cry." Reid leaned closer. "I have to do some work when we get back to my place, but I can cook us something for dinner first."

"Or we could grab something on the way home and you could finish your work before *Game of Thrones* comes on."

Reid gave Zeke another kiss. "Good idea."

Chapter Six

Monday morning, Kade sat at the kitchen table with Jace. "I have a favor to ask."

Jace glanced up from his coffee cup. "Shoot."

"I talked it over with Lark, and he thinks we should stay in town for the rest of the week and head back on Sunday." It had been Lark's suggestion, and Kade had fought him over it for close to an hour, but, as usual, Lark had finally worn him down.

"Fine by me. If you want, you can use the cabin at the lake. I'm in back-to-back meetings all week, so we'd already planned to stay in town."

"Thanks." A week at the lake would be perfect. It would give Kade a chance to get to know Zeke better and mend a few fences with Lark at the same time. "I'd definitely like to get some fishing in."

Jace chuckled. "Just make sure Lark uses one of my cheap poles this time."

"Hey," Lark said, coming into the kitchen. "You told me the one I lost was a cheap one."

"I lied. You were too cute and embarrassed to be told how much it really cost. Besides, I didn't know you as well back then." Jace refilled his cup and added a teaspoon of sugar.

"Oh, I see, now the dirty truth comes out." Lark sneered at Jace in a mocking way. He turned his attention to Kade. "Does the talk about fishing mean we're going to spend some time at the cabin while we're here?"

"Yep."

"Cool." Lark shifted from side to side. "In that case, I'd like to run out and get a few things, including a small rental car for me to drive while I'm here."

"I've got the bike," Kade reminded Lark.

"I know, but there're some people I'd like to catch up with while we're here. You'll probably spend most of your time with Zeke anyway," Lark argued.

"You're right." Kade finished his coffee. "Give me two minutes to put my boots on."

* * * *

Fresh from the shower and dressed only in a thick terry robe he'd borrowed from Reid, Zeke left the apartment and went downstairs. He found Reid hard at work in his office, looking as sexy as he had an hour earlier when he'd fucked the hell out of Zeke's hole. "Kade just called. Lark has a few things he wants to do while they're here, so they've decided to stay the rest of the week."

Reid set down his pen and sat back in his chair. "Does that mean I'll get to spend the rest of the week with you?"

Zeke hoped Reid would want to do more than that. He moved Reid's papers and sat on the desk. "Well, I hope so. The thing is, the week's up on my motel room tomorrow, and I was kind of hoping you'd let me stay here with you."

Reid ran his hands up Zeke's thighs and under the robe to his cock. "I'd love to have you in my bed all week."

Zeke watched as Reid slowly separated the terrycloth. "I thought you had a ton of work to do?"

"I do." Reid buried his face against Zeke's balls. "But I also know that at any minute Kade could call and steal you away from me for the day."

Zeke leaned back on his forearms and watched Reid lick and kiss his cock. "Actually, I thought, after you got your paperwork finished, you and I could go out and do something."

Reid licked a pearl of pre-cum off the crown of Zeke's dick. "I'd love that. What'd you have in mind?"

"I don't know, I thought maybe you could show me around town or something. It's a gorgeous day outside. If you hurry and finish in time, we could even go to lunch and I could give you a hand job under the table or something."

Reid moaned. "You know me too well already." He sucked the tip of Zeke's cock into his mouth just as his cellphone rang.

Zeke picked it up and looked at the display. "It's Rick."

Reid released Zeke's cock with a curse. He took the phone from Zeke. "Hey."

Zeke sat up while Reid talked to his brother.

"He hasn't called. He's probably trying the old number again. I've told him a dozen times to have one of you program my new one into his phone." Reid rolled his eyes and shook his head. "I'll call him, but promise me you'll change his phone next time you're over there." He nodded. "Okay. Love you. Talk later." He hung up. "Sorry, I need to call my dad."

"I understand." Zeke scooted off the desk. "I'll get dressed and go check out of the motel while you make your call and finish the books."

Reid stood and pulled Zeke against him. "You look good in my robe."

"I try." Zeke chuckled. He opened his mouth for a deep kiss from Reid. When he felt Reid's cock harden, he broke the kiss. "You'd better make that call."

Reid ran a finger up and down the crack of Zeke's ass. "I'd guess I'd better before I bury my tongue in that pretty hole of yours."

It was Zeke's turn to moan. Reid was by far the most adventurous lover he'd ever had, and Zeke was quickly becoming addicted to it. He stepped out of Reid's embrace before he bent himself over the desk and spread his butt cheeks. Begging had never been one of his strong suits, but he'd do it for Reid's talented tongue. "Later," he said before leaving the office.

Zeke was headed toward the door that would lead him to Reid's apartment when he heard a knock on the front door of the club. He closed the robe and retied the sash before going to investigate. *Lark?* Zeke unlocked the front door. "Hey."

One look at Zeke in his bathrobe and poor Lark turned bright red. "Sorry. Am I interrupting something?"

"Unfortunately, no. Reid's on the phone with his dad." Zeke walked toward the bar. "Can I get you something to drink? I can make coffee."

"Orange juice?" Lark asked.

"Sure." Zeke went behind the bar.

"How's the hand doing?"

Zeke glanced down at the bandage. "I wouldn't even notice it if I didn't have to stick my hand in an empty bread sack just to take a shower." He smiled. "So what's going on?"

Lark sat on one of the stools. "I'm out doing some grocery shopping for the cabin, and I thought I'd take a chance and stop by. We haven't really gotten the chance to talk one on one."

"Okay." Zeke poured them each a glass of orange juice before moving to sit next to Lark. He tucked the robe between his legs in hopes of maintaining a portion of modesty in front of his brother's partner. "Do me a favor and tell Jace and Sam thanks again for the party yesterday. It was nice being able to meet your friends."

"With a little time, they could become your friends." Lark sipped his juice. "This is good. Fresh?"

Zeke laughed. "No. Hell, for all I know it may have some vodka mixed into it."

Lark looked at his juice again. "Do you really think so? It's bad enough that I'm drinking the juice, Kade'd have my balls in a sling if he thought I was drinking alcohol, too."

Zeke knew Lark had some kind of blood sugar problem, so he decided to stop fucking with him. "Don't worry, there's nothing but juice in your glass."

Lark pushed the glass away. "I've probably had enough anyway." He clasped his hands and rested them on the bar. "I thought I'd ask if you could use an impartial sounding board."

"About?" Zeke probed.

"What's going on with Kade and Reid."

Zeke finished his juice. "And how can you be an impartial sounding board? You sleep with my brother every night."

"Doesn't mean I agree with him every night," Lark shot back.

Zeke narrowed his eyes. "Maybe I'm confused. What exactly are we talking about? Is Kade still feeling weird around me?"

"No, Kade's having some jealousy issues with you and Reid, and I suspect Reid's feeling the same about Kade," Lark explained.

"That's stupid. They mean two different things to me." Zeke had suspected Reid had felt left out the previous day, but jealousy over Kade simply didn't make sense to him. "Unless Kade's into some freaky shit. That's not it, is it?"

Lark's eyes rounded behind his glasses. "No!" He covered his mouth and started to giggle. Honest to God, the man was giggling. "Sorry, no, that's not it. I meant Kade wanted us to go home this morning, taking you with us, before you could spend more time with Reid. He's afraid Reid will convince you to stay here in town."

"I don't—" Zeke began, but Lark cut him off with a hand in the air.

"I told Kade he was being an asshole. I also told him that the decision was yours to make, and if he wanted to do what was best for you he'd give you the chance to spend more time with Reid to see if it leads anywhere."

"And that was enough for him to change his mind?" The Kade that Zeke had known growing up had been a stubborn son of a bitch. He couldn't imagine Kade changing his mind so quickly.

"Almost. I told him that I was staying until next weekend, so unless he wanted to go back without me, he'd keep his cute butt right here." Lark grinned. "I've learnt to pick my battles with your brother, so when I argue with him about something like this, I usually win."

When Zeke had first met Lark, he hadn't been able to picture the small nerdy-looking guy with Kade, but he saw it now. There was something incredibly irresistible about the quiet man. "Next time you stand up to Kade, can you wait until I'm in the room?"

Lark's grin got even wider. "I'll try."

* * * *

Zeke couldn't get the conversation with Lark off his mind as he walked, hand in hand, with Reid. They'd been in several clothes stores, and, although Reid had tried to get Zeke to look at clothes, he wasn't interested. Clothes had never meant anything to him other than something to cover his body to avoid arrest.

"Let's go in here," Reid suggested, opening the door to an antique shop.

Zeke cringed but followed Reid inside. He clasped his hands in front of him and tried his best not to touch anything. It was amazing the way Reid thought nothing of picking stuff up to get a closer look.

"Feel how worn and soft this wood is," Reid said, holding out a long bowl.

"No, thanks."

"You don't have to worry about breaking it."

"I'm not. It's—it used to belong to someone else. Every time I see this stuff it makes me sad to know that the only reason it's probably here is because someone died and their loved ones didn't care enough about their stuff to keep it." Zeke nodded toward the bowl. "Like that. I'm sure that used to sit on someone's table or something. They had to have either made it or saved money to buy it, and I'm sure it meant something to them. They die—the kids come in and sell everything for a few bucks." He shook his head. "It bothers me."

Reid studied the bowl for a few moments. "Yeah, I guess I can see that." He set the bowl down. "I've never thought of it that way, but it makes sense now that you've pointed it out. The only problem is that the family has already gotten rid of it. So people, like me, buy it and enjoy it for another fifty years or so. I like the thought of someone enjoying the things I love even after I'm dead and buried."

It was Zeke's turn to look at the bowl in a new light. He thought of all the things he'd left behind when he'd taken off after Kade. He knew Isaiah had cleared the house out and sold it, but he'd never asked what had happened to the stuff inside. His dad had had a nice pipe collection, and even though it had meant absolutely nothing to him, he wondered if someone had found the perfect pipe amongst his father's to complete their particular collection. It was a nice thought. "Okay, I get it when you put it that way."

"And that, my sweets, is why no two people are exactly the same. Wouldn't it be a boring world if we were all clones of each other?" Reid questioned.

"It'd be like having sex with yourself. Although that's not always a bad thing, but I'd probably be happier if all clones were built like you. Actually, now that I think of it like that, hell, I'd be playing with myself all day." He winked at Reid before wandering down the aisle.

Reid caught up with Zeke so they could finish touring the shop. Zeke felt better about being surrounded by dead people's things, but the only thing he wanted to touch was Reid. While Reid checked out an antique cash register, Zeke began to roam Reid's ass with his palms.

"Having fun back there?" Reid asked.

"I can't seem to help myself. It's like your ass is made of steel and my hands are big magnets," Zeke explained.

"I *knew* those *Buns of Steel* workout tapes would eventually come in handy."

Zeke gave Reid's ass another squeeze. It had been the best day, and they hadn't even had lunch yet.

* * * *

"I hate fish," Zeke complained as he swung his legs over the end of the dock. "About six years ago, I was between jobs and camping out with a sleeping bag I bought from a second-hand store. For almost two weeks, all I had to eat was the fish I happened to catch each day."

"So you were homeless?" Kade asked, his eyebrows drawing together in a scowl.

"No more than I've been the last ten years. Whether you're sleeping in a hotel bed or on the ground, neither of them would qualify as a home." Suddenly uncomfortable with the topic, he reeled in and cast his line again for something to do.

Kade set down his pole and got to his feet. "You want a bottle of water?"

"Sure." Zeke wondered if Kade thought he was a pathetic excuse for a man. Tired of fishing, he pulled in his line before placing the borrowed pole back in the shed. He decided to save Kade a trip and went to the house.

Crossing under the open kitchen window, Zeke overheard Kade talking to Lark. "He slept on the fucking ground for weeks."

Before another word could be uttered, Zeke jogged to his Harley. He felt like a loser as it was, he sure as hell didn't need to hear his own brother talking about it. Pulling out of the graveled drive, he tore out and headed for Reid's place. It may not have been his home, but Reid always made him feel as though he belonged.

The entire ride to Reid's was a blur of emotions that swung from pissed off to hurt to resolved. He parked in his usual spot and used the key to the side door that Reid had given him earlier.

After a quick check of Reid's office, Zeke went upstairs. He knocked once before opening the door. "Did ya miss me?"

Stretched out on the couch watching television, Reid sat up and smiled. Reid's joyful expression at Zeke's early return said more than words ever could. "Hey."

Zeke kicked off his boots and launched himself onto the couch. "I missed you."

Reid wrapped his arms around Zeke and gave him a deep kiss. "Kade called. He got worried when he heard you ride away without saying goodbye."

"I don't want to talk about Kade right now." Zeke climbed off Reid. "What I want to do is get naked and order a pizza," he said as he began to undress.

Reid pulled off his T-shirt and pushed down his sweatpants. "Would you get the stuff out of the bedroom?"

Zeke thought about it for a minute before shaking his head. He stretched out on top of Reid and sighed. "Can we just lie here together and watch TV for a while?"

"Sure." Reid handed Zeke the remote. "If we lie here long enough, will you tell me what's bothering you?"

"I told Kade something that I wasn't proud of, but I was trying to open up and let him into my life." Zeke glanced at Reid. "Within minutes, he told Lark. So now Lark knows what a loser I am, too."

Reid didn't say anything. He simply wrapped his arms around Zeke and offered comfort. *Perfect.* It was exactly what Zeke needed and wanted.

Zeke gave Reid the remote back. "You can watch it. You're all I want right now." He closed his eyes and held onto the solid man under him. They both had to be downstairs for work in two hours, but until then, he planned to try to figure out what it was he wanted. Kade and Lark were leaving in three days. A big part of him didn't want to go to Cattle Valley with them, but he hadn't known Reid long enough to move in. He thought of the savings account Isaiah had set up for him after he'd sold their family house. He'd always sworn to himself that he wouldn't touch the money until he'd found Kade and was ready to settle down. With Kade located, Zeke still needed to figure out where he'd settle down and if he was even ready to give up the carefree lifestyle he'd grown accustomed to.

Watching one of the twenty-four-hour news channels, Reid casually rubbed his palm against Zeke's back. The fact that the comforting gesture wasn't at all sexual in nature warmed Zeke more than anything Reid could've said. It was at that moment that he realized their new relationship wasn't all about sex. While the fucking was out of this world, Reid actually liked him, and Zeke felt the same way.

"Have you ever owned a house?" Zeke asked.

"Sure." Reid put down the remote and held him with both arms.

"Is it worth the money to buy versus rent?" Zeke was embarrassed he didn't know the first thing about either one, but he didn't believe Reid would think less of him for it.

"Depends on who you talk to, I guess. In this economy, the monthly payment's about the same. Although you have to do regular maintenance on a house, you get to make it your own in a way that you can't with a rental. It also depends on how long you plan to own the house. If you're looking for a place for a few years, it doesn't make sense unless you're in a great market."

Zeke thought of the yellow house that had captured his attention a few days earlier. Hell, he'd received twelve stitches because he hadn't been able to take his eyes off the place when they'd walked by. "I think I'd like to buy one," he confessed. "I don't know if I have enough money, but I saw one the other day that I'd like to look at."

"Here in town?" Reid asked, his hands coming to a full stop.

Zeke shrugged, unsure how to take Reid's reaction. "Is that a problem?"

Reid sat up as though he didn't have a hundred-and-seventy-pound man lying on top of him. "How can you ask me that? It's everything I want, but I thought you were determined to go home with Kade. Is this about what happened today?"

Zeke thought about it. "Yeah, but not for the reason you think."

"Okay, what's the reason?" Reid asked.

He was about to open himself up again. Zeke prayed it wasn't shoved back in his face. "When I overheard

Kade talking to Lark about me, the only thing I wanted at that moment was you. I couldn't get here fast enough, and, as you know, it had nothing to do with your incredibly sexy body. It was you and the way I feel when I'm with you that I craved at that moment."

With Zeke settled on his lap, Reid leaned in for a deep kiss. "You can stay here with me."

"Thanks, but, although I already know I'll be spending a lot of time here, I want a house." Zeke didn't tell Reid that he was afraid in six months he'd get the itch to check out the next dot on the map. A house would ground him, something he knew he needed. Solitude had been his drug of choice for years. It was easy to blame everyone else for his problems when he was alone, and he was sure that at some point in the future he'd freak. It might be a stupid argument with Reid or something at work, but he would definitely get the urge to bolt, something he couldn't really do if he had a mortgage to consider. "And I think I'd like to get a dog, and maybe a truck."

Reid's brow furrowed. "That's a lot of changes to make after such a short time. Maybe you should take things one step at a time."

"Are you afraid we'll break up and I won't want to be here anymore?" Zeke couldn't understand Reid's unease.

"It's not about breaking up. It's about overwhelming yourself. I think if you change your life so drastically without giving yourself a chance to assimilate to a new way of living, you'll be setting yourself up to fail. I don't want to lose you because of that. I'd rather see us get to know each other better and maybe, eventually, we could buy a house together."

"What about a dog? That would probably keep me here if I get the itch to leave." Zeke needed something to ground him. Sure, maybe buying a house on a whim wasn't the smartest decision, but what could be the harm in using a dog to do the same thing?

Reid deposited Zeke—none too gracefully—onto the couch before standing. "So, all this buying a house, getting a dog, it's all about keeping you here?"

"Yeah," Zeke replied, unsure of what was about to happen between them.

"I want to be enough to keep you here, and if you don't think that'll happen, that I'm *not* enough, then why would you want to tie yourself to this town?"

Fuck. He'd hurt Reid again. "I've never had the desire to do anything remotely like this. I've never fallen in love with someone. So, don't get your feelings hurt every time I question if I'm capable of doing it in the first place. It's one of the reasons I thought I'd just go with Kade. I. Do. Not. Want. To. Hurt. You," he said, enunciating each word.

Reid dropped down beside Zeke. "You love me?"

"Yeah, I think so, but that's part of my problem. I don't have anything to base this feeling on. I don't know whether it's real or if it'll last. I'm used to fucking guys and moving on." Zeke took a deep breath. "For the first time in my life, I don't wanna go anywhere and it scares me."

"I don't want you to leave, but I want to be the reason you stay because I'm stupid in love with you."

Zeke could barely draw air into his lungs at Reid's proclamation. *I'm loved.* He wrapped himself in the words and gave them time to settle into his soul. "In six months, we get a dog."

Chapter Seven

Kade leaned against the bar. "Are you ever going to talk to me?"

Zeke finished pouring a round of shots for Kade's table. "I'm working. We can talk later." He held up the tray. "Do you want to take this with you or do you want Jeremy to carry it to your table?"

Kade was frustrated. He'd tried to talk to Zeke numerous times since he'd left the cabin, but each time he'd gotten Reid on the phone, he'd been told Zeke was busy. "I've been trying to talk to you for hours. When's later?"

Zeke glanced at the small digital clock behind the bar. "I've got a dance in a few minutes, but I'll take a break after that. Is that good enough?"

"You're acting like a brat," Kade said. It would be different if he knew what he'd done to piss Zeke off enough for him to leave without saying goodbye but he didn't. How was he supposed to fix the problem if he didn't know what the hell it was? He picked up the tray. "Let me know when you can squeeze me into your schedule."

Zeke immediately moved away to take another order from Jeremy, and Kade carried the drinks back to the table.

Lark waited for Kade to sit down before snuggling against him. "Did you talk to him?"

"He's busy, but he said he had a break coming after his dance."

Sammy sat up straighter. "He's getting ready to dance?"

"That's what he said." Other than the video on Lark's phone, Kade hadn't seen his brother in action, but he'd been the talk of the bar all night.

"I think you should find someplace else to be when that happens," Jace told Kade.

"Why? I thought you said he left his clothes on." Kade would go ape-shit if he found out his baby brother was stripping for Reid.

"Believe me, it has nothing to do with taking his clothes off. Last time we were here, Sammy made me follow him into the bathroom to fuck him. Do you have any idea how long it's been since Sammy begged me for sex in a public place?" Jace leaned over and kissed Sammy. "And that's exactly why I'm not planning to miss a second of Zeke's show."

Sammy hit Jace's forearm. "Look, he's cleaning off the bar."

Jace tipped his shot of tequila against Kade's glass. "Trust me. Go to the bathroom or something."

Kade upended his own shot and let the alcohol slide down his throat. He decided to take Jace's advice. "Okay." He stood and almost made it to the hall when *I'm a Slave 4 U* by Britney Spears started to play. Kade turned and watched Zeke jump onto the bar, shocked at what came next. Sex seemed to ooze from Zeke's pores as he gyrated to the music.

"Fuck," he spat out as he turned and marched down the hall. Instead of going to the restroom, he knocked on Reid's closed door. The music and crowd were so loud by that point that he couldn't hear anything else. He eventually opened the door a crack. "Can I come in?"

"Sure." Reid gestured to one of the chairs. "I take it from the catcalls that Zeke's doing his thing."

"Yeah, which is what I wanted to talk to you about. How can you claim to care about him and let him do something like that? Don't you realize every man in that room is thinking of nothing but fucking him?"

Reid grinned. "The fact that I'm in love with Zeke has nothing to do with him revving up the crowd. He does it because he gets one hell of a lot of money, and he likes the way it makes him feel when people watch him." He held up his hands and shrugged. "I'm not worried about anyone fucking him. He's mine, and I make sure everyone who steps foot in this bar knows that."

Alec had briefly mentioned Reid's particular kink, but Kade had never thought his baby brother would be into something like that. "I don't think you're a very good influence on Zeke."

"I don't give a fuck what you think. Zeke's been dancing on tops of bars for years, long before the two of us got involved."

"I'm not just talking about the dancing. Alec told me you get off on some kinky shit and it didn't matter at the time because you weren't doing it to my brother, but now that you are, it matters. You're practically prostituting him out when you let others see him like that," Kade argued.

Reid leaned forwards and rested his arms on the desk. "I appreciate that Zeke's your brother, and because of that I'm not going to kick your ass out of my club, but I am telling you to get the fuck out of my office. When you open your sex life to me and my opinions, I'll take what you have to say into consideration, but I don't take that shit from my friends and family, and I sure as hell won't take it from you."

Kade's hands curled into fists. If Reid wanted to fight, he was ready.

The door opened and Zeke stepped inside. His gaze went from Kade to Reid and back to Kade. "What's going on in here?"

"Your brother was just leaving," Reid growled.

Zeke walked over to Reid and gave him a kiss. "Would you mind if Kade and I used your office to talk?"

Reid stared up at Zeke for several moments before nodding his agreement. "I'll be behind the bar if you need me."

"Love you," Zeke whispered to Reid.

The sentiment was loud enough for Kade to hear, leaving him stunned. Reid had already told Kade that he loved Zeke, but it wasn't the same as knowing Zeke loved Reid back.

Reid kissed Zeke again before walking out of the office. Zeke immediately turned on Kade. "What the fuck went on between the two of you?"

Kade refused to be intimidated by Zeke's icy glare. "I told him I didn't approve of him or his lifestyle, at least not where you're concerned." He crossed his arms. "Now, tell me why you left the cabin the way you did earlier today?"

"Because I overheard you telling Lark how disgusted you were that I spent a few weeks sleeping on the ground," Zeke shot back. "And if you're mad at me for leaving, fine, but don't you dare take it out on Reid."

"First of all, I wasn't disgusted that you slept on the fucking ground, I felt bad because I know why you did it. Secondly, my beef with Reid is his desire to have sex with you in public. That's not okay with me."

"I don't give a fuck what's okay with you. What goes in my ass and where I am when it happens is not your business. I may've needed your advice on sex when I was going through puberty and just figuring who I was, but you weren't there, remember? So, I sure as hell don't need it now."

Kade took a deep breath. He'd been surprised that Zeke hadn't been angrier with him than he'd seemed to be that first night they had talked. Now, he realized Zeke had a great deal of anger buried inside him. "Don't stop there — tell me what you really think."

"I think you're a selfish prick who only cares about yourself."

"How do you figure that? I spent years feeling guilty because I was afraid I'd gotten you into trouble for blaming you for the shit that went down with Dad."

"Again, about you. If you'd really given a shit about me, you would've at least tried to call me to make sure I hadn't received the brass end of Dad's belt after you left."

"Did you?" Kade asked. He'd been on the receiving end of that big heavy buckle, so he knew what kind of damage it could do.

"No, although I think that would've been better than being ignored every fucking day after you left. Dad shut out everyone, including Mom. Life sucked after you left, so I clung to the belief that you would've taken me with you if I hadn't been so much younger."

Kade's anger dissipated. For the first time it wasn't the image of himself riding away from Zeke that haunted him, but rather what had come after. Zeke was right—the years he'd spent reliving that one day centered on how it had made him feel to accuse Zeke then leave him. "I'm sorry that I wasn't there to help you through stuff."

Zeke sat in Reid's chair. "Yeah, I'm sorry, too." He rocked back in the chair and stared up at the ceiling. "I'm glad I kept looking until I found you, but now that I have, it's time I find myself."

"By staying here with Reid," Kade surmised.

Zeke met Kade's stare. "Yes. I don't expect you to understand my relationship with him, but he calms the drifter in me. For the first time in my life, I want to stay and learn everything there is to know about someone."

"I thought you wanted to get closer to me? Isn't that why you've been searching all this time?" Kade questioned. He was losing his brother, and he knew it.

Zeke stood and crossed to stand in front of Kade. He gave Kade a hug and continued to hold on. "Now that I've found you, I won't let you run off on me again, but that doesn't mean I want to share your life. That belongs to you and Lark. It's time I got my own."

Kade rested his cheek against Zeke's head. "Lark and I come down every couple of months."

"I'm counting on it."

"I'm not sure if Reid and I will ever see eye to eye where you're concerned," Kade admitted.

"You will if you take sex out of the equation, and see him for the man he is. He loves me, and I've never known a more caring man."

"Promise me one thing?" Kade asked.

"What?"

"Next time I come back to this bar, you'll give up dancing for the night. I swear I may be scarred for life."

"As long as you promise to take good care of yourself. I know you have your health under control, but you have to realize I'm going to worry about you for the rest of my life."

Kade chuckled. "Funny, I was just thinking the same thing about you."

"Guess that means we're really brothers again."

* * * *

Reid was sitting at one of the back corner tables, sipping cranberry juice and ginger ale, when Zeke rang the 'last call' bell beside the bar. He'd wandered out of his office thirty minutes earlier and had joined Alec, Max, Tony and Daniel at the same table Kade had sat at a few hours earlier.

"Boy, he hits that bell and this place really starts to clear out," Alec pointed out.

"That's why he does it." Reid glanced across the room at Zeke. He wasn't sure what had gone on in the office between Zeke and Kade, but when they'd both come out, Zeke had been in a decent mood and Kade had stopped long enough to shake Reid's hand before he'd left for the night.

Zeke said something to Wyatt before walking toward Reid. "Hey," he said straddling Reid's lap. He sat down and leaned in for a kiss. "I told Wyatt if he loaded the glasses, I'd do everything else behind the bar."

Reid pushed the back of Zeke's shirt up and began rubbing the soft skin at the base of his spine. In their current position, the low-rise jeans made it possible for Reid to run his finger up and down the top half of Zeke's ass crack. "So you decided to come over and join our little party?"

Zeke moved closer to Reid until he was grinding against Reid's cock. "It looked like the five of you were getting bored. But I can leave if I'm interrupting something."

Reid looked around Zeke to his friends. They were transfixed and Tony had pulled Daniel onto his lap and Alec had Max tight against him. "I don't think they mind."

Zeke continued to grind against Reid as he kissed and licked Reid's ear. "Did I tell you I caught Wyatt with Jude earlier?"

"What do you mean you caught them?" It was one thing for him to fuck on company property, but he wouldn't have it from his employees.

"The two of them were all hands and mouths with each other in the kitchen. It was before we opened, but it still surprised me. I've seen Jude watching Jeremy a lot, but I had no idea he was into Wyatt, too."

Reid worked Zeke's zipper down and stuck his entire hand down the back of Zeke's jeans, trying to get to the hole he knew was already lubed for him. "Keep an eye on it for me. I have the feeling Wyatt knows his way around a bedroom, but I doubt the same could be said for Jeremy. If you see either Holt or Jude making a play for Jeremy, let me know."

Tony stood and pulled Daniel to his feet. Their erections were obvious and both looked like they couldn't wait to fuck. "I think we're going to take off."

"I'm glad you stopped by," Reid told them without taking his hands off Zeke.

"Later," Tony said to Alec before leading Daniel away.

Zeke moaned and rocked back on Reid's long middle finger. "You want to lay me on the table and fuck me right here?"

"Of course I want to, but I won't while we're still open." Reid made eye contact with a heavy-lidded Alec. It was obvious by the way Max's arm moved that Alec was getting a hand job under the table. "You enjoying yourself, buddy?"

"I may have found a new favorite place to take Max for date night," Alec replied, his voice laden with arousal. He looked up at the ceiling. "I'd like to hire someone to build a partition or screen for this section? All clubs need a VIP section and this corner would work perfectly."

Reid grinned. Alec was more like Reid than he cared to admit. "Sure, I'll try to find someone."

Zeke moaned loud enough that it caught Jeremy's attention as he was bussing tables. Reid watched as Jeremy tried to work out what he was seeing. Jeremy's gaze landed on the hand shoved down the back of Zeke's jeans and the way Zeke was rocking back and forth. Jeremy's plump pink lips opened slightly as he looked mesmerized by what was happening at the next table.

When Zeke cried out and shoved his hand between him and Reid to touch his exploding cock, Jeremy's big blue eyes became even bigger. *"Wow,"* Jeremy mouthed. It wasn't until that moment that he noticed Reid watching him. He quickly grabbed the big plastic tote of glasses and scurried off toward the kitchen.

"You've damaged that boy for life," Alec proclaimed.

Reid shook his head. "He seems hungry for knowledge. I just hope he finds the right guy to teach him."

"Oh, fuck," Zeke gasped, collapsing against Reid's chest. "It's been a while since I've come in my jeans." He lay in Reid's arms for several minutes before sitting up. "I'd better get to work or we'll never get to bed."

"Do me a favor and check on Jeremy."

Zeke looked confused. "Why?"

"He just witnessed our little show, and I'd like to make sure I don't lose a good server because of it."

A sparkle lit in Zeke's eyes. "He saw us?"

Alec laughed. "Look around, there're about ten horny guys staring at this table."

Zeke licked his lips. "Cool." He climbed off Reid's lap and reached for a pile of cocktail napkins.

Reid rolled his eyes as Zeke took his time cleaning the cum from his cock and stomach. "I've created a monster."

Zeke was still laughing when he zipped up and walked off.

* * * *

Reid pulled the Escalade to a stop in front of the cabin on Sunday morning. "This is a nice place."

Zeke climbed out and waited for Reid to join him. "Jace and Sam stay out here a lot in the summer, I guess." He knocked on the front door and waited.

"Good morning," Lark greeted with a big smile. "Breakfast'll be ready in about fifteen minutes," he said, leading them to the kitchen.

"Where's Kade?" Zeke asked. When Lark had called to invite them to breakfast, he'd confided to Zeke that he was worried. Kade had a history of debilitating depression, and Lark was afraid the love of his life was traveling down that path once again.

Lark pointed out of the window. "He said he wanted one more cup of coffee by the lake."

Zeke filled a cup from the pot on the counter. "I think I'll join him." He gave Reid a quick kiss before pushing open the back screen door. "Mind if I join you?" he asked, drawing closer to Kade.

"Not at all." Kade gestured to the picnic bench beside him. "There're a couple swans out there this morning."

Zeke straddled the bench and sat sideways facing Kade. "As long as they stay over there, I'm fine. They may be pretty, but they're mean as hell."

"Yep."

Zeke tapped his fingers against the side of his cup. "Are we okay?"

Kade finally looked away from the water. "Yeah, we're solid. It'll take me some time to come to terms with everything I put you through by leaving, but I'll get there."

Zeke scooted closer to Kade and rested his forehead against Kade's biceps. "Don't. We need to both let it go. Mire yourself in the past and you'll be too screwed up to enjoy the present." He grabbed Kade's hand with both of his. "I'm excited by the prospect of starting a new life here with Reid. I want that. I think I deserve that. But I can't fully enjoy it if I know you're killing yourself with guilt. Please, Kade, be happy for me."

Kade nodded. "I am happy for you."

"But you're not happy for yourself. You have something you didn't have a week ago. Me! And if you're a glutton for punishment, I bet you can even reconnect with Isaiah, although I have to tell you the man is completely boring and full of himself."

Kade chuckled. "Sounds like the Isaiah I remember."

"Oh, he's worse, believe me." Zeke grinned. "But he's still a Straus, so I suppose we should eventually invite him to Thanksgiving or something."

"I'd like that."

"Reid asked me this morning if I'd be interested in going to Cattle Valley Days this year." Zeke released Kade and took a drink of coffee.

"He knows about that?" Kade asked.

"Yeah. He's been poring over the town's website. Making plans and stuff. It's important to him that you and I build a strong relationship." Zeke hoped Kade could forget the sex stuff that he didn't approve of and get to know Reid.

Kade nodded and tipped his cup back. "You ready for breakfast?"

"I'm starving," Zeke said, standing.

"Don't get your hopes up. I love Lark to death, but his idea of breakfast and my idea of breakfast are two different things. His real name is Meadowlark—he grew up in a commune in Canada, all healthy, free love—total wackadoo lifestyle."

Zeke laughed and bumped against Kade as they walked to the house. "I'll pretend that I love what he's made even if I don't like it."

"Good. That's what I do, too. Although take my advice and don't make too big a deal out of any one thing because then he'll cook it every time you come down."

"Duly noted."

Epilogue

A month later, Zeke had been promoted to floor manager, and he swore it had absolutely nothing to do with him getting fucked by the boss several times a day. Zeke was damn good at his job and he'd worked at enough bars over the years to know how to handle the various situations that came up.

Jeremy set a glass on the bar in front of Wyatt. "According to table six, this tastes like horse cum. How he knows that, I don't know, and I was afraid to ask."

From his position a few feet away, Zeke tried to keep from laughing. He'd become a huge fan of Jeremy and his subtle, awkward humor.

"Fuck 'em," Wyatt said. "There's not a damn thing wrong with it."

Zeke wasn't sure what was going on with Wyatt lately, but he was definitely off his game. Instead of listening to Wyatt bitch for the next hour, Zeke grabbed the glass and took a drink before it was poured out. He spat it back into the glass without swallowing it. "I'll take the gentleman at table six's word for it. That is probably the nastiest thing I've ever put into my mouth." He picked up a napkin and did his best to wipe the taste from his tongue. "What'd you put in that?"

Wyatt stared at Zeke with a blank expression. "A simple black Russian."

Zeke shook his head. "That was tequila in that glass, not vodka." He slapped Wyatt on the back. "Make him another one and give it to him on the house."

"Problem?" Reid asked from the end of the bar.

"Nope." Zeke turned away from Wyatt and joined Reid. "What're you doing out of your office?"

"Kade called. He wants to know if you'll ride one of his custom Harleys in the parade next weekend."

Plans had been finalized for their first trip to Wyoming for Cattle Valley Days, and Zeke couldn't wait. He'd purchased a cowboy hat and a pair of chaps that had already been put to use. "Is he riding in the parade, too?"

"Yeah. He said there'd be five of you all on his custom bikes that he hasn't sold."

"Sure. I'd—" Zeke broke off when he spotted a disturbance at table six. "Son of a bitch." He rounded Reid at a fast clip and stormed toward the asshole who had Jeremy pinned to his lap. "Holt!" Zeke yelled above the music.

By the time Zeke had reached the table, Holt already had the fucker face down on the floor. "You okay?" he asked Jeremy.

Jeremy was trying to straighten his ripped T-shirt. "I'm sorry, Zeke, he just grabbed me like that when I told him his drink was on the house. He said he'd rather pay for the drink and get a little something extra from me. Next thing I knew he'd grabbed me and pulled me into his lap."

Reid leaned over and said something to Holt that Zeke couldn't hear. Holt nodded and pulled the man to a standing position by the scruff of the neck.

"Get Jude to take his picture before you toss him out," Reid told Holt. He stood in front of the man who had terrorized Jeremy and pointed a finger in his face. "If you ever show your face in this bar again, I'll let Holt take you out back and show you how we deal with trash." He stepped back. "Get him outta here."

Zeke wrapped an arm around Jeremy and led him to Reid's office. "We'll get you a new shirt." He eased Jeremy down onto one of the chairs before going to the closet where the boxes of shirts were stored. Being manhandled in a bar was fairly common, but he could tell by the freaked expression on Jeremy's face that it had been his first time. "Small or extra small?"

"Small's fine."

Zeke pulled a fresh shirt out of the box. "Catch." He tossed it to Jeremy. "You okay?"

"My dad bought me a Taser when he found out I was working in a bar. I thought he was being typically overprotective." Jeremy turned his attention to the small rip in his jeans. At least that hadn't been caused by the asshole, it was a fashion thing. "If it's okay with Reid, I'd like to bring it with me tomorrow night."

"I'll talk to him about it, but I think he'd rather have Holt or Jude deal with that stuff. From what I understand, you can seriously injure someone with a Taser. It'd be one thing if you were walking on the sidewalk or something and someone was attacking you, but because you're at work, it's our job to make sure you're safe."

Jeremy took his shirt off. "What should I do with this one?"

Zeke tore his gaze away from the tiny silver hoops in Jeremy's nipples to take the shirt and toss it into the trash can. "Nice tan," he commented.

"Since I decided to skip summer classes this year, I've been spending a lot of time lying out with a few of the other guys at BK House."

"BK House?" Zeke questioned. Was Jeremy really in a fraternity?

"It's a private dorm for gay students off campus. Tony helped get it built."

The office door opened and Holt stuck his big, chocolate-brown, bald head inside. "He's gone," he told Jeremy.

"Thanks, Holt." Jeremy stood and pulled on his fresh shirt.

Zeke grinned at the hungry expression on Holt's face. He knew Reid didn't want Holt messing around with Jeremy, but he had a feeling Reid's request had more to do with Holt's attachment to Jude. At least Zeke and Reid agreed on the fact that Jude was a player. What the hell Holt saw in him no one understood. No one except for Wyatt, of course, who had been fucking Jude behind Holt's back since the club opened.

"Did you ride your bike to work again?" Holt asked Jeremy.

Jeremy nodded. "I don't like to take the chance of missing the bus."

"I'll put your bike in the bed of the pickup and give you a ride back to the dorm after work," Holt offered.

Zeke knew he should intervene, but Holt appeared to be almost as shaken as Jeremy had been. "Probably a good idea. At least for a few days."

"Okay," Jeremy agreed, tucking in his shirt.

"Drink orders are backing up." Reid stepped into the office. "Everything okay in here?"

"Yeah. I gave Jeremy a new shirt." Zeke gave Reid a quick kiss. "Back to work." He left the office, nudging Holt out of the door with him. He assumed Reid would want to ask Jeremy a few questions about what had happened and maybe file some kind of incident report.

"Thanks for offering to give Jeremy a ride home." Zeke slapped Holt on the back. "You're a nice guy for a giant."

"Don't thank me. If Reid hadn't stopped me tonight, I'm not sure what I would've done to that guy."

"That's why it takes all of us to calm a situation like that down." Zeke broke away from Holt and went back to work.

* * * *

After five hours on the road, Reid pulled into a gas station. "You going in?"

Zeke yawned and stretched his arms over his head. "Yeah, I feel the need for Funyons and a big bucket of Coke. What about you?"

Although Funyons weren't his favorite road-trip food, it would help in the kissing department if they both had onion breath. "Same."

Reid got out of the Escalade and started filling the tank. Nine hours might be too long of a drive for him more than once or twice a year. He hadn't checked into airfare because Kade and Lark made it sound like the trip was a breeze. Wrong.

Zeke came out of the store carrying two extra-large drinks and a big bag of Funyons. He set the items in the car. "Be right back. There's something I want to show you." He took off again before Reid could question him further.

Reid finished pumping the gas and stood beside the bumper waiting for Zeke. He remembered that movie about the woman who had been abducted from a gas station and buried alive. *I watch too many movies.*

Zeke came into view from around the side of the building. He was carrying a puppy. Fuck. Reid held up his hands. "Zeke, we talked about this."

"I know, but oh my God, look at this cute little face." Zeke held the puppy out toward Reid. "Feel how soft he is."

Reid rubbed the dog's ear. "What kind is he?"

"The guy said he wasn't sure what the dad is, but the mother's a sheltie. I guess she was a tramp and got out of the yard when she wasn't supposed to." Zeke held the puppy in front of his face and rubbed noses with it.

Reid couldn't decide which was cuter, the damn puppy or the way Zeke acted around the puppy. "We don't have a yard, so you'll have to take it for a walk several times a day. It might sound okay this summer, but come winter and you'll be sorry."

"She, not it." Zeke laid the puppy against his chest. "Please. We've been talking about getting a house anyway."

Damn, why did he find it so hard to tell Zeke no? The answer came to him immediately—because Zeke rarely asked for anything. "Fine," Reid said. "We'll need to find a store or something and get her a leash and collar before we get much farther."

Zeke tilted his chin up and gave Reid a kiss. "I love you."

Reid opened the passenger door for Zeke and their newest roommate. "Love you, too." He shut Zeke's door before going around to the driver's side. "So, have you given her a name yet?"

"No. I thought I'd let her pick her own name. She'll do something over and over again and we'll know what to call her."

"As long as she doesn't end up with a name like Puddles, or Chewy, I can live with that." Reid pulled out of the parking lot, a smile on his face. Life didn't get any better.

COMING CLEAN

Dedication

For Kristina Galbert. Thanks so much for all your support.

Chapter One

Chase Hughes stared at the large flat-screen television in the BK House rec room without seeing a damn thing. The phone in his hand dropped to the sofa cushion beside him. He needed to get off the couch and jump into the shower before work, but he couldn't get the conversation with Benny, his boyfriend of two years, off his mind.

It wasn't that the phone call had been bad. He never had a problem talking to Benny because they knew each other so well they never ran out of things to say. Nope, it was the way Benny ended their daily calls with an 'I love you' that made him feel like shit.

Benny Allenbrand was one of the nicest guys Chase had ever known, and there had been a time when the two were inseparable, but that had been before Chase had gone off to college. Being two and a half years younger, Benny wouldn't graduate high school until May.

Chase glanced at the phone. Benny had accepted a scholarship to play football for North Central Idaho University. The same football team Chase played on.

It had always been their plan for Benny to graduate and join Chase, so what the fuck was wrong with him now that their dream was going to come true?

Wyatt came into the room, twirling a set of keys on his finger. "Do you still need a ride to work?"

Chase glanced at the clock. *Fuck.* So much for getting a shower in. He got to his feet and stretched his arms over his head. "Do I have time to change?"

"Sure. I thought I'd grab something to eat from the kitchen before I left anyway. Meet you back here in fifteen?"

"Great." Chase picked up his phone. He should have enough time for a quick shower. It was his first night back to work since he'd returned from winter break and he couldn't wait to get some money in his pocket again. He'd only worked at Clean Slate since he'd turned twenty-one in November and couldn't believe the bar's owner, Reid, had given him time off to go home for Christmas.

It only took Chase a moment to race to his room and grab a towel and his shower bucket. He stripped out of his clothes and stepped under the hot spray of water. When he'd first taken the job at Clean Slate, he'd made piss poor tips until Wyatt and Zeke had clued him in on what to wear and how to flirt. He still wasn't as good as Wyatt and Zeke at the flirting, but he'd spent his entire first week's pay on clothes that he wouldn't be caught dead in back home in Cattle Valley.

After a quick scrub, Chase spent a couple of minutes getting his blond hair styled. He preferred the just out of bed look and obviously, so did the bar patrons, because the less time he spent on it, the higher the tips.

Chase pulled on his low-rise jeans and tight white T-shirt with the bar's logo. Wyatt had told Chase he'd make even more money in tips if he got his nipples pierced, but he wasn't willing to go that far. He was the smallest quarterback in the college's history and was already pushing his luck with the football team. Showing up for spring training with pierced nipples would likely get him jumped in the showers.

Fully dressed, Chase stopped by his room to toss the towel toward his bed and retrieve his wallet. "I'm going to work," he told his roommate.

Rusty glanced up from the book he was reading. His parents had died in an accident less than six months earlier, so Rusty had stayed at BK for the holidays. Chase couldn't imagine how shitty that would be.

"Okay," Rusty replied before going back to his book.

As Chase jogged down the steps, he prayed he wasn't the only student who'd come back from break early. A packed bar was a lucrative shift.

* * * *

"This place is dead," Skeet Drews declared, entering the garage through the tiny showroom.

Mac glanced up from the custom bike he was working on. "Not many people are out looking for Harleys when there's a foot of snow on the ground."

"So why're you even open? Knock off early and let's grab a drink." Skeet plopped down on one of the small metal stools Mac had sprinkled around the three bay garage.

Mac didn't dare tell his best friend that being alone at the shop was a hell of a lot easier than being alone at home. He'd made the mistake of letting Skeet talk him into going to Clean Slate a few months earlier, and Skeet hadn't shut up about going back since. "That place is too loud."

"Fuck, when did you become an old man?" Skeet tapped a booted foot against Mac's workbench.

"When I became responsible for a wife and son at the age of eighteen, asshole." Mac returned his attention to the gas tank he'd been grinding on.

"Who said anything about getting drunk? I figured we'd have a couple beers, a big plate of chili cheese fries and maybe get lucky."

Mac didn't bother to reply. He liked a good hard fuck as much as the next guy, but knew from experience he couldn't find what he was after in a damn bar. It was probably a sick fucking thing, but he enjoyed the chase. Unfortunately, the guys that seemed to slither over to him when he was at a club only wanted one thing. Where was the challenge? He needed a challenge. He fucking lived for it. His dick wouldn't even get hard unless he believed he was about to tap something special. Still, it was almost seven and the thought of going home didn't hold much appeal.

"Come on. I don't want to go by myself," Skeet begged.

Mac growled as he set the hand-grinder aside. One of the advantages of owning his own custom motorcycle shop was the ability to set his own hours, and since he hadn't had a single customer all day, he decided to follow Skeet's lead. "You start turning off the lights while I get things locked up."

Skeet clapped his hands. "That's what I'm talking about. You won't be sorry."

Skeet's enthusiasm was not infectious, leading Mac to think he was already sorry he'd agreed to the night out.

* * * *

"Hey," Chase answered his phone. He nodded when Zeke indicated the tray full of drinks on the bar.

"You have time to talk?" Benny asked.

"Sorry, I'm in the middle of my shift. Is something up?" Chase tucked the phone between his cheek and shoulder while he added slices of lime to two of the beer bottles.

"Not really. I can't stop thinking about our call earlier."

Chase squeezed his eyes shut. "Why don't I give you a call back on my break?"

"When's that?"

Chase glanced at the large clock over the bar. "Another hour and twenty." Discussing their earlier conversation wasn't something he felt like doing on his break, but he knew Benny wouldn't sleep until they'd worked things out between them. Chase still wasn't sure he was doing right by Benny and had said as much hours before.

"I guess," Benny mumbled.

Zeke gave Chase a look that said Chase better get the fuck off the phone and do his job. "Okay, gotta go or I'll lose my paycheck."

"Sure." Benny sighed. "I love you."

"Yeah." Chase winced. Once again, it was the awkward part of their conversations. He hung up and stuffed the phone in his bar apron. "Sorry about that."

Zeke poured another draft beer and set it on Wyatt's tray. "Don't let Reid see you doing that." He grinned. "I'm the nice one."

Chase loved his boss, so he doubted that was the truth. He rolled his eyes and picked up his order. "But he's the hot one," he replied in total honesty. Reid was gorgeous, and Chase often found his gaze straying to the older man when he was in the room.

"Watch it," Zeke warned. He winked at Chase and gestured across the bar with his chin. "You've got a new table."

Chase groaned. His station was already loaded. Who the fuck knew that so many people would take refuge in a fucking bar during a snowstorm? He could kick himself for hoping the bar would be busy. It seemed fate had been listening. Balancing the tray, he turned and caught sight of the bar's newest refugees. "Fuck me." He barely caught his tray before it toppled to the floor.

Zeke started laughing. "Yeah, I thought you'd say that."

Both men were hot, but one in particular was every daddy fantasy Chase had ever had. Clad in a skintight black Under Armour shirt, the patron's muscular chest and arms were on glorious display. There was a hint of a tattoo on the man's throat with even more ink showing on his forearms and wrists where the long-sleeved shirt was pushed up.

Chase wasted no time delivering the drinks, so intent on getting to the hot guy that he didn't even bother to flirt. He approached the high top table and prayed his voice wouldn't crack but was thankful he wore the short apron that hid his raging erection. *Shit.* The man's nose was fucking perfect. "Welcome to Clean Slate," he greeted. "What can I get you?"

The gorgeous one, the one with the devilish dark brown beard and big hazel eyes, grinned at him. *Fuck.* Chase thought he'd die right there in the middle of the packed bar. "Haven't seen you before," the man replied, his voice so deep Chase felt it vibrate his fucking balls.

"I haven't been here long." Chase tucked the tray under his arm. "I'm Chase." Although he had other customers to tend to, he wanted to milk his moment with the hot hunk.

"Chase," the man repeated with a nod. "I'm Mac and this is my friend Skeet."

Chase flicked a glance to Skeet before returning to Mac. Sure, Skeet was handsome too, but he didn't have that bad boy look that Mac had in spades. "Nice to meet you." He smiled, knowing his dimples would be on full display.

Mac held Chase's gaze for several beautiful seconds. "Two glasses of Sam Adams," he eventually said. "And two orders of the chili cheese fries," he added.

"That it?" Chase asked. "You look like a man who enjoys a good steak, and Raul has some delicious New York strips in the kitchen."

Mac looked to Skeet. "You need to get home for any reason?"

Skeet shook his head. "Medium-well for me with a loaded potato."

Chase nodded and waited for Mac to order. "What kind of vegetables do you have tonight?"

"Ummm." Chase thought for a few moments. "Steamed broccoli or green beans," he recited, getting lost in Mac's hazel eyes. It was rare, extremely rare, that a man affected him to the point where he couldn't think.

"Great. Medium-rare with a side of the broccoli," Mac replied.

"Do you still want the chili cheese fries?" Chase knew he was stalling, but he didn't want to walk away.

"Yeah, give us one order. We can share it while we're waiting for our meal."

"Sure thing." Chase smiled again, wondering what Mac's hair looked like under the black beanie. "Be right back with those beers."

"I'd say take your time, but I'm very thirsty," Mac said with a wink.

Chase tore himself away from the table. He pulled his order pad out of his apron and wrote up the food order. He dropped it off with Raul before stepping up to the bar. "Two Sam Adams," he told Zeke.

Zeke eyed Chase as he filled two glasses from the tap.

"What?" Chase asked, feeling uncomfortable. "I'm flirting. Isn't that what you told me to do? Besides, I have a boyfriend back home." He didn't know who he was trying to convince, Zeke or himself. *Benny.* He inwardly groaned.

"You have that look on your face when you're around that boyfriend of yours?" Zeke set the glasses on Chase's tray.

"What look?" Chase knew for a fact Zeke couldn't see the erection still pressed against his fly.

Zeke shook his head and picked up a rag to wipe off the bar. "Never mind."

Chase stood staring at Zeke for several moments. "Whatever," he grumbled, picking up the tray. On his way to Mac's table, another of his regulars called out to him.

"Hey, QB, get us another round."

"Sure thing." Chase tried to remember what the table of football fans were drinking. Mac had him so wound up his memory was shit. "Here you go," he said, arriving at Mac's table.

"QB?" Skeet questioned.

"I'm the Big Horn quarterback," Chase explained, setting Skeet's beer on the napkin he'd laid out.

Skeet punched Mac in the arm. "Hear that?"

Mac nodded. "Yep."

Skeet gestured to Mac. "He rarely misses a home game. His son plays high school football in Los Angeles."

"Fuck!" Mac turned to Skeet. "You gonna give the kid my whole fucking history?"

Chase felt like he'd been slapped. *Kid?* Evidently he'd been wrong about the mutual attraction he'd felt between them earlier. He took a step back, taking himself out of the line of fire. "I'll bring those fries out as soon as they're ready." Then, with his virtual tail between his legs, he got the hell away from the table.

* * * *

Mac jabbed the last of the fries with his fork. He was in a bad mood and wished to hell he hadn't put in the order for dinner. All he wanted was to get the fuck away from Skeet and the blond-haired temptation that had refused to even meet his gaze when he'd delivered the fries.

"You're an asshole," Skeet said, wiping his mouth.

Mac glared at Skeet. He loved his friend and would do anything for him, but, Jesus, he'd been riding a pretty fucking awesome high before Skeet had put the brakes on things by reminding him of Jackson.

The QB had been into him, Mac knew that much, and for a while, he'd let himself believe he'd had a chance. It had been a long time since he'd fucked. Not because he hadn't had volunteers. Nope, the problem was all his. He was the kind of man who didn't take someone home to fuck unless he was really attracted to them, and in nearly a year, not one sonofabitch got his dick hard. *Until Chase. Fuck!*

"What? You got nothing to say?" Skeet pushed. "I saw the way you looked at him."

"Leave it," Mac warned.

Skeet drained the last of his second beer and held up his hand to get Chase's attention. "If you're not gonna make a move, I am."

"Leave it," Mac growled, repeating himself.

Skeet fucked anyone who gave him a second look, male or female. The thought of Chase getting mixed up in Skeet's frightening love life didn't sit well with Mac.

Mac chanced a glance at Chase as he approached the table. He met Chase's gaze before Chase quickly broke eye contact and suddenly realized it wasn't disinterest Chase had in his eyes, it was fear. What the hell? He mentally replayed their earlier conversation in an attempt to figure out what he'd done to give Chase the impression there was something to fear from him.

"Two more?" Chase asked Skeet.

"Yeah," Skeet answered.

"I'll check on your food, too." Chase retreated without looking at Mac.

Mac had spent the better part of his adult life knowing his size and looks intimidated most people, but, usually, after someone gave him a chance to talk, they were quickly put at ease. It appeared he had the opposite effect on Chase and he didn't like it one bit. He zeroed in on Chase's ass as the quarterback walked to the food service window cut into the wall. *Fuck.* He couldn't get past that look of fear in Chase's big blue eyes.

"You okay, man?" Skeet asked, interrupting Mac's train of thought.

Mac knew in his gut he wouldn't be okay until he figured out what the hell had happened, but he wasn't about to tell Skeet that. "Yeah."

"I was just messing with you when I said I'd make a move on the quarterback."

Mac glanced at his best friend. "You've known me since kindergarten. Have I ever, in all that time, given you the impression that I liked being messed with?"

"No, but I've also never known you to shy away from what you want." Skeet leveled his gaze on Mac. "I thought you were all about the hunt. You're not too old for him if that's what you're worried about."

It wasn't the age difference that bothered Mac. Hell, the way Chase affected him, he wasn't even sure he needed the hunt. It was something else entirely. When Skeet had stupidly brought up Jackson earlier, Mac had been pissed. Chase had quickly backed away, and, at first, Mac thought it was because Chase had realized how much older Mac was, but he no longer believed that was the case. "He's afraid of me now," Mac growled.

"Although that would make sense since you're a scary-looking motherfucker. I didn't get that vibe from him when he came over and introduced himself. I thought he was into you." Skeet looked over his shoulder at Chase. "But now that you mention it, he does seem different than he was a half hour ago."

Yeah. Mac tried to relax his scowl as Chase made his way toward the table with a large tray laden with dinner plates, steak sauce and two frosty glasses of Sam Adams.

"Sorry it took so long. It seems everyone's hungry tonight," Chase said as he started emptying his tray.

"That's okay," Mac replied, trying like hell to keep his gravelly voice easy. He knew his voice intimidated many people, maybe that was Chase's problem.

Before Mac could think of something else to say, Chase set the fresh beer in front of him. "I'm going on a short break, but I'll check back with you in a few minutes. In the meantime, if you need anything, just flag down Wyatt," Chase said, holding the empty tray at his side but avoiding eye contact.

Shit. Mac knew he had to set the situation right before he left.

* * * *

Chase stacked the tray on the stand outside the food window. "I'm taking a short break," he informed Zeke, grabbing his coat from behind the bar. He made his way through the crowd to the front door.

"You leaving?" Holt Graves, one of the Clean Slate bouncers asked.

"Just getting some fresh air." Chase opened the door and squinted against the cold and blowing snow.

"You're crazy," Holt replied.

"Yeah, I am." Chase moved around the side of the building, hoping to block most of the wind, and pulled out a pack of cigarettes. He didn't smoke a lot, mostly at work, and never during football season, but he found it calmed him.

It took Chase several moments to light the damn thing, but eventually he was able to take his first deep draw. "Fuck yeah," he mumbled to the snowflakes raining down on him. He fingered the phone in his pocket, knowing he needed to call Benny, but feeling too strung out to deal with it.

Before leaving for college, Chase had sat Benny down and they'd discussed the fact that an exclusive relationship couldn't work when they were so far apart. He'd thought Benny had understood and agreed to the arrangement, but Benny's guilt trips were getting worse all the time.

When Chase had gone home for winter break, he'd promised himself he'd break it off with Benny completely. He didn't know how it had happened or when, but he'd changed somehow and had discovered his feelings for Benny weren't the same as they'd once been. Unfortunately, Benny was still, and would always be, one of the nicest guys Chase had ever met. Hurting someone with a heart as big as their six-foot-five frame wasn't an easy thing to do. So, he'd left Cattle Valley without gathering the courage to let Benny down easy. Even the thought of a confrontation with Benny made Chase sick to his stomach. He pulled out his phone, and tried to gather the courage to use it. Benny wouldn't be put off, Chase knew that from experience. If he didn't call him now, Benny would blow up his phone with texts and calls until Chase had no choice but to answer it. Of course, by then, his usually sweet Benny wouldn't be so sweet. Nope, that wasn't something he was willing to get into.

"I thought I saw you come out here," Mac said, rounding the corner.

Chase shoved his phone into his coat. He stared at Mac for a brief moment before holding up his cigarette. "I'm sneaking a smoke."

Mac dug into the inside pocket of his thick leather coat and withdrew a pack. "Mind if I join you?"

Chase glanced down at his cigarette. "Guess not." He returned his gaze to Mac. "Something wrong with your food?"

"Seems my appetite left me." Mac used his coat to block the wind as he lit his cigarette. "I wanted a chance to apologize for whatever I did or said earlier to scare you."

"You didn't," Chase was quick to say, even though it was a damn lie.

Mac stared at Chase as he inhaled. "Yeah I did, and if it was because I snapped at Skeet, you can't take that shit personally. I don't like to be reminded of a son who no longer wants anything to do with me." He blew a cloud of smoke into the air. "I've been sittin' in there thinking about it, and I realized that things were going good until that part of the conversation went down."

Chase watched as the smoke seemed to dance around the falling flakes. He didn't want to talk about it, but he didn't want Mac to feel guilty for something that wasn't his fault either. "I don't handle confrontation very well, unless it's on the football field. I never have. It's something I hate about myself, but can't seem to do anything about." He flicked his cigarette into the street before pulling out a roll of mints. He stuck two in his mouth. "Want one?"

Mac tossed his half-smoked cigarette. "Sure." He followed Chase's lead and popped a couple of mints into his mouth. "I'm too old to beat around the bush about shit like this, so I'll ask you straight. You seeing someone?"

Chase was shocked. The gorgeous man in front of him was still interested. He closed his eyes, wanting so much to tell Mac the absolute truth, but feeling guilty because he hadn't even told Benny the truth. "Kind of." He shrugged. "Back home."

Mac shoved his hands in his pockets. "All right."

Shit. Shit. Shit. Chase didn't want a chance at Mac to slip out of his fingers. He sighed and shook his head. "It's not all right at all, but I'm too much of a pussy to do anything about it."

Mac's brows rose, moving his black beanie higher on his forehead.

Chase took a step forward. He stared into the warm depths of Mac's hazel eyes that were more green than brown. Never in his life had he been so drawn to someone, so fucking hard just from looking at them. He wasn't sure what was happening between them as they stood, staring at each other in the freezing night air, but his want for Mac scared him. Given the shit he still had to deal with, the last thing he should do was act on his attraction, but he couldn't let the moment pass without at least knowing what those damn lips felt like. He took several steps and surprised himself, and Mac it seemed, by placing a soft kiss on Mac's lips. *Fuck!* "I'd like to explain the situation, but if I don't get back to work, Reid'll can me," he whispered. Before he could pull away, Mac wrapped his arms around him and pulled him closer.

Mac narrowed his eyes as he stared down at Chase for several heartbeats before kissing him again. He parted Chase's lips and thrust his tongue inside, thoroughly mapping the inside of Chase's mouth. Unlike Chase's kiss, Mac's was consuming, branding, and when he eventually broke away, Chase was left breathless. "Call me if you get the situation with your boy back home worked out."

"I don't have your number," Chase replied. The desire to lick his lips and taste Mac again threatened to overwhelm him. He waited two heartbeats before giving into the compulsion.

Mac's lips parted slightly as his gaze seemed to zero in on Chase's tongue. He cleared his throat. "You can reach me at Mac's, the custom bike shop here in town."

Chase had passed the shop several times. "I've seen it. The bus route goes right by that place on the way to the mall."

Mac reached out and brushed the pad of his thumb across Chase's lower lip. "Goddamn, you're young," he mumbled.

There were many things about himself that Chase had figured out since moving away from home, and one of those, the one that had the potential to hurt Benny the most, was his attraction to older men. It didn't necessarily make sense, given that his own father had been such an asswipe, but Chase was drawn to mature men. Real men with muscles and tiny lines around their eyes and strands of gray in their hair. Men who had learned how to fuck a man from experience instead of watching free porn on the internet.

Fuck! Chase couldn't let Mac walk away. "I told Benny when I left for college that I wanted to date other people," he blurted out.

Mac grunted. "If all you want is a hard fuck that's good enough for me." He brushed Chase's lip again. "But, if you want something more, you'll have to be honest with me, yourself and your friend back home." He dropped his hand. "Think about it."

Chapter Two

Mac mentally kicked himself in the ass as he sat in a booth against the wall after waving to Chase. It had been a week since he'd tasted Chase, and no matter what he did, he couldn't get the sexy fucker off his mind. He'd told himself he'd wait for Chase to make up his mind about the guy back home, but here he was, ready to help speed up the process. As a rule, young guys weren't his thing, too many games. Chase came with a shitload of problems, and if Mac hadn't seen firsthand what the brief argument between him and Skeet had done to Chase, he would've believed Chase was playing games. Unfortunately, Mac had seen the scared expression he'd witnessed on Chase's face before, and the knot in his gut wouldn't let him just walk away. The kiss they'd shared continued to haunt him. Goddamn. He needed more of those fucking kisses.

Clean Slate was empty except for a few tables. It was barely five, too early for a crowd and the main reason Mac had closed the shop early. He wanted a few minutes of Chase's time without worrying he'd get the guy fired.

"Hi, Mac," Chase greeted, walking toward the table. "Sam Adams?"

"Sure." Mac crossed his arms and rested them on the table. He knew he was staring at Chase, but he couldn't tear his eyes off him. He didn't know how it was possible, but Chase looked even hotter than before.

"You need a menu?"

Mac shook his head. "I've already got plans for dinner."

"Oh." Chase's expression fell. "I'll get that beer."

Mac wasn't used to telling people his schedule, but it was obvious Chase thought he had a date and that wouldn't do. The only date he wanted was one with the man in front of him.

"Here you go." Chase placed the beer in front of Mac. "Would you like to run a tab?"

"No thanks." Mac handed Chase a ten-dollar bill. "You got a minute?"

Chase studied the bar before nodding. "Until someone else comes in."

Mac didn't want to come right out and tell Chase what his plans were so, he improvised. "You have desserts here? I'm going to Skeet's sister's house for the weekly family dinner and thought I'd bring something sweet."

Chase's face brightened. "Yeah. Raul made some Bourbon Bread Pudding, or, there's also some cherry cobbler."

"Sounds good." Mac mentally calculated numbers in his head. "Give me five of the cobblers to go before I leave." Mac took a sip of his beer. He'd never been good at small talk, but he wanted to get to know the younger man. "So, where're you from?"

After another quick glance around, Chase slid into the booth across from Mac. "I was born in Seattle, but Mom moved us to Cattle Valley when I was in the eighth grade."

"Cattle Valley? That town in Wyoming?" Mac shook his head. As a gay man, he'd heard of the small town that was like the Holy Land for the LGBT community, but he'd never been there.

"Yeah. It's a great place. You been there?" Chase asked.

"No. I'm from LA, so this is as small town as I get." Mac took another drink. "The thought of everyone knowing my business gives me the creeps."

Chase shrugged. "Guess it depends on what you're after. It made me feel safe."

Mac's chest squeezed. "That's nice."

"It was except..." Chase shook his head as he snapped his mouth shut.

"Except what?" Mac pushed.

Chase sighed and rested his head on his hand. "It's hard to be an individual when everyone in town knows you. I go back now and I'm known as half of Benny and Chase. I can't talk to anyone without them asking where Benny is. What's worse is that once I talk to Benny, I'll be known as the asshole who broke Benny's heart."

Mac reached across the table and rubbed a finger up and down Chase's forearm. It was a stupid gesture, but he wanted to touch Chase more than he needed to breathe. "You don't have to live in a small town for that situation to occur. Except for Skeet and his sister Evie, I don't have a single friend from LA who'll still talk to me."

"Why?" Chase asked. He lowered his arm and threaded his fingers through Mac's.

Mac wasn't ready to spill his guts on his past. He'd eventually have to tell Chase he'd had a stupid moment of clarity and had come out to his wife without knowing his son was standing in the doorway. He'd lost his house, his business and his family all because he didn't want to die with a lie on his tongue. "I got into a wreck that fucked me up for a while." He met Chase's gaze. "Messy divorce followed, and my son sided with my ex," he finally answered. "I haven't seen him since the day I left her."

Chase nodded. "My parents' divorce was messy, too."

Mac was relieved Chase had brought up the subject. "Do you see your dad?"

"No," Chase was quick to say. "And I hope I never do." He withdrew his hand. "I'd better get back to work. Do you want another beer?"

Mac knew he'd lost Chase for the time being. "Just the cobbler."

* * * *

Chase stared at the twenty-dollar bill in his hand as he laid in bed. The only light on in the room came from Rusty's desk lamp. Rusty, his roommate for the year, was a walking, talking brain, and although he wasn't the funnest guy to hang around, he was always willing to help Chase with his homework. He groaned when a text came through, knowing it was Benny.

"That bad?" Rusty asked, glancing over his shoulder to look at Chase.

"I'm a failure as a boyfriend," Chase declared.

Rusty turned in his chair to face Chase. "I thought you were going to talk to Benny when you went home for Christmas?"

"I was, but he was so damn sweet the whole time I was there." Chase dropped the twenty on his chest before reaching for his phone. For two weeks, he'd stared at the hastily written phone number on Mac's generous tip, wishing like hell that he could man-up and tell Benny the truth.

Rusty pushed his wire-framed glasses up on his nose. "Isn't sweet what most guys dream of?"

"Yeah, and that's part of the problem. I know I should be madly in love with Benny. He's hot as hell, sweet, funny and kick-ass on the football field. He should be the perfect man for me, but he doesn't make my stomach flip when I'm around him."

"Flip?" Rusty questioned.

Chase glanced at his roommate. Rusty was one of the sweet ones like Benny. He was cute with his small size, dark red hair and smattering of freckles that ran across the bridge of his nose, but he wasn't Chase's type. Hell, as far as he knew, Rusty didn't even date, so he wasn't sure Rusty understood the reference. "Have you ever met someone that made you feel like you were either going to throw-up or strip your clothes off?"

Rusty bit his bottom lip before turning back to his homework. "Only once, but I've found that feeling to be superficial."

"Better superficial than to be with someone you love but don't desire," he mumbled. "And, for the record, it has nothing to do with how handsome someone is. I think it's a chemical thing or something. All I know is that I want to be with someone who turns my insides out."

Rusty didn't say anything more, and Chase wondered if he'd struck a nerve. He shrugged and read the text.

Hey, when u come home for Spring Break, would u bring me a T-shirt from the bookstore on campus?

Chase took a deep breath before texting back.

I'm not going home for Spring Break because I need to work, but I'll send u one.

Really? Maybe I should ask Dad if I can come up there? Benny replied.

"Fuck!" Chase spat. "Benny wants to come here for Spring Break."

"That's two months away," Rusty noted.

"Yeah, but Benny will start planning now if I say okay." Chase sighed. "If he starts planning, he'll be even more heartbroken when I get the nerve to tell him I'm not in love with him anymore. Hell, maybe I never was."

When Rusty didn't reply, Chase glanced up from his phone. "What do you think I should do?" he asked Rusty.

"I don't know. My dad always told me to make decisions based on what kind of man I wanted to be, but that doesn't really fit the situation. I mean, while I hate to see you hurt someone as nice as you say Benny is, I wonder what'll do more damage, hearing the truth now or eventually finding out you lied to him for so long."

Chase's thumb hovered over the keypad for several moments as he thought about what Rusty had said.

Hold off on the plans. Mine might change between now and then.

He hit send and closed his eyes.

"There's this guy that's come into the bar that makes my insides quiver." Chase had no idea why he was spilling his guts to Rusty. Maybe it was the low lighting or the fact that he needed someone to talk to and Rusty was handy.

"I assumed the twenty meant something special when you were too broke the other day to go out to eat with the other guys because you refused to spend that one," Rusty said.

Chase dropped his phone to the bed. He retrieved the twenty from his chest and stared at the masculine handwriting. "It's driving me crazy. Mac's dropped by Clean Slate three times since the first night I met him. He comes before the crowd so we have a chance to talk."

"And?"

"I really like him, but the first night I met him, I found out he's not allowed to see his son." *Fuck.* Chase couldn't get beyond that information. Even if Benny was completely out of the picture, he wasn't sure he should pursue Mac.

"And, you're afraid it's for the same reason your mom moved you to Cattle Valley." It wasn't a question.

Evidently, Rusty was a good person to talk to because Chase had shared a ton of shit with his roommate. "Yeah." Chase fingered the small scar on his cheekbone.

"Ask him," Rusty suggested.

"I can't just come out and ask him something like that." Chase's phone buzzed again. He glanced at the display.

Okay, let me know. Love u, B.

Chase turned his phone off and plugged it into the charger beside his bed.

Chase stared up at the ceiling, remembering the volatile man he'd grown up around. Ken Hughes had been a monster of epic proportions, and Chase couldn't stop worrying about the old saying of girls being attracted to men like their fathers.

Chase rubbed his eyes before they had a chance to fill with moisture. He'd cried a lifetime's worth of tears over the hand he'd been dealt as a kid.

"Chase?" Rusty cleared his throat. "Not all men are like your father," he said, his voice so soft Chase barely heard him.

"I don't want all men. I want Mac," Chase said with a sigh. "I just have to figure out whether or not I'm willing to risk everything for the chance to find out what kind of man he is."

* * * *

Mac stared at the phone on his desk. "Goddamn you, Skeet," he mumbled, angry at his best friend for bringing up Jackson. It had been almost six months since he'd tried to get Jackson to talk to him. Six months since he'd been turned away for the millionth time. "Fuck!"

Legally, Jackson didn't have to talk to him, but Mac had always remained hopeful that once his son got older, he'd be given a chance to explain his side of the story. Of course, that was never going to happen if Jackson continued to refuse his calls.

Snatching up the phone, he called his ex-wife. She still lived in the house Mac had bought, and had painstakingly refurbished. The killer was that she now lived with her new husband in that damn house. *Butch.* Mac shook his head. The fucker had been one of his best friends. Janice had moved Butch into the house so fast, there was no way they'd started dating *after* Mac had asked for a divorce.

"Hello?" Janice answered.

"Hey." Mac waited a heartbeat before continuing. "Jackson there?"

Janice sighed. "He doesn't want to talk to you. Why won't you get that through your head?"

"Did he get the Christmas present I sent?" Mac asked.

"You need to stop sending him things. It confuses him, and he's impossible to live with for days afterwards," Janice replied. She sighed again. Hell, Janice was always sighing about something. "Mac, the judge said it was up to Jackson whether or not to see you and he doesn't want to. If I need to take you back to court, I will."

"I guess you're gonna have to because the custody agreement didn't say anything about me contacting him, only that you were granted sole custody with no visitation on my part," Mac growled. He wondered what had happened to the sweet girl he'd grown up with. The beautiful girl he'd thought could change him. *Shit.* Like always, the call only depressed him further.

"Will you at least tell him I called?" Mac needed Jackson to know he'd never give up.

"Goodbye, Mac," Janice replied before hanging up the phone.

Exploding out of his chair, Mac hurled the handset across the showroom floor.

"Wow!" Evie exclaimed. "Telemarketer?"

Mac put his hands on his hips and took a deep breath, trying in vain to calm his racing heart before he scared the shit out of Dillon and Emmy. He plastered a smile to his face and greeted three of his favorite people in the world. "Oops it slipped right out of my hand."

Emmy, Evie's four-year-old daughter, picked up part of the broken phone. "It's broke."

"Yeah." Mac chuckled. He pointed to the trashcan beside her. "Would you do me a favor and throw it away?"

Happy to be given a task, Emmy dropped the largest chunk in the can before going back for more.

Mac held out his arms. "Give me that big boy."

Evie handed eighteen-month old Dillon to Mac. "I warn you, he's due for a nap."

Mac blew a raspberry on Dillon's chubby stomach. "Hey, Bubba."

"Don't call him that," Evie whined, taking a seat. She dropped her purse and diaper bag on the floor. "Whew, it's a madhouse in here."

Mac chuckled. The small showroom didn't get a lot of foot traffic. Most of Mac's sales were done either online or through custom orders. It was fine with him. He'd rather have ten people a month who were serious customers over a hundred jackasses just looking. He only had one part-time employee, which kept the overheads low, and gave Mac the freedom to spend the majority of his days in peace. "It's quiet. Just the way I like it."

Evie pulled a ponytail holder off her wrist and gathered her long black hair high at the back of her head. "You going to tell me what that tantrum was about?"

Emmy tugged on Mac's jeans.

Mac slid his bottom drawer open, and Emmy immediately started to dig through the toys he kept for her and Dillon. Evie was Skeet's sister and the two of them were the closest thing he had to a family. "I tried calling Jackson," he admitted.

Evie's expression fell into pity. "Oh, Mac." She stood and came around the desk. Taking off his standard black beanie, she kissed the scar on the top of his head "Why? You know it messes you up for months every time you try."

Mac rubbed his lips against Dillon's soft cheek. "I can't stop hoping, sweetheart." The thought of never wrapping his arms around his son again was enough to bring tears to his eyes. "I haven't heard his voice in eight years. You have any idea what that feels like?"

Evie pressed her cheek against the top of Mac's head. "I can't imagine." She nuzzled his head again. "Maybe once Jackson gets out from under Janice's thumb, he'll realize you're not the bad guy."

Fuck! Mac handed Dillon back to Evie. He could feel himself sliding into the black hole he'd lived in for years. When the present he'd sent Jackson for Christmas hadn't been returned like all the others, he'd foolishly hoped his son was ready to talk.

"You want to come by tonight for dinner?" Evie asked, replacing Mac's hat.

"Thanks, but there's someone I need to talk to." Maybe staring into Chase's big blue eyes would help. Even though he'd told Chase he wouldn't pursue him until after the situation with the hometown boyfriend was taken care of, Mac wanted him. Hell, he couldn't get the damn QB off his mind and had damn near become a regular at the bar because of it.

"Emmy, put the toys away. We have to get home and make dinner for Daddy." Evie rolled her eyes. "Emmy's decided she wants to be a chef like the ones she sees on TV."

"I'll remember that next time I drop by the toy store." Mac smiled at Emmy. Christ he loved that little girl.

"Don't get drunk tonight," Evie said, shaking her finger at Mac.

Mac refused to make that promise. "If I do, you don't have to worry about me driving." His hands shook, the wounds too close to the surface to joke about.

Evie gave him a kiss on the cheek. "Call me or Skeet if you need a ride."

If luck was on his side, Mac knew Chase would be driving him home. "I will. Love you."

"Love you!" Emmy yelled, blowing kisses as she giggled.

Mac leaned down and scooped the girl into his arms. "Love you, too, Bug."

Emmy continued to giggle as Mac peppered kisses to her face and neck. He set her down and pinched her nose. "You'd better get home and cook dinner." He got another round of kisses before Evie and her tiny gang left the store.

Mac smiled, his heart full of love for the woman and her children. After the divorce, it was Evie who had suggested he and Skeet move to Idaho. Evie's husband, Ron, had believed in Mac enough to help set him up with the shop once he'd arrived.

Mac closed his eyes and pictured the lucrative business he'd built in Los Angeles. With over twenty employees, Mighty Mac's had been the shit for people who were into spending a ton of money on their rides. He shrugged to himself. Just plain Mac's wasn't nearly as big or prestigious, but it gave him comfort and a place to create while making a living. He'd be forever grateful to Evie and Ron for helping him gather the upfront money. It was because of his friends that he'd been given a second chance at life, and as he pondered his night ahead, Mac decided he'd waited long enough to taste Chase again.

* * * *

"Chase! Clean Slate's on the phone," Rusty said, his voice echoing in the large communal bathroom.

Chase stepped into the spray and washed the soap from his body. "I'll be done in a minute. Ask who it is and tell 'em I'll call them back." He gave his dick one last tug before shutting off the water.

"It was Zeke. He said that biker guy's at the bar asking about you."

Chase grabbed his towel and slid the shower curtain open. "No shit?"

Rusty made a face and turned his head. "Put your junk away."

Laughing, Chase wrapped the towel around his waist. "Give me the phone."

Rusty handed Chase the phone. "He didn't say it was an emergency. I'm sure you can dress before you call back."

Chase glanced down at his tented towel. The mention of his sexy biker had his cock predictably hard. "Believe me, if Mac's at the club and interested enough to ask for me, it's an emergency." He grabbed his shower bucket as he called the bar.

"Clean Slate," Zeke answered.

"It's Chase. Would you ask Wyatt to tell Mac I'm on my way?"

Zeke chuckled. "Better get here quick. The vultures are starting to circle."

"Shit. Just tell him I'll be there as soon as I can." Chase ended the call. He looked at Rusty. "Can you give me a ride? The bus'll take too long."

"I have to study," Rusty argued.

"It's Friday night. You have all weekend to study," Chase reminded his roommate.

Rusty bit his bottom lip. "I've never even been inside a bar."

The admission shocked Chase. He'd planned on having Rusty drop him off, but the chance to see Rusty watching one of Zeke's late-night shows was too much to pass up. "One beer. Hell, one Coke."

Rusty took a deep breath. "Thirty minutes."

"Fantastic."

* * * *

"They really need more security lighting in their parking lot," Rusty complained as he locked his car.

Chase nodded absently, his mind on spending time with Mac. He wondered if the biker danced. The thought of pressing against Mac to the beat of the music hardened his cock again. *Fuck.* His body was out of control.

"Do I have to pay to get in?" Rusty asked.

"No, but you'll have to show your ID." Chase grinned at his roommate. "Seeing as how you look like you're around sixteen."

Rusty surprised Chase by giving him the finger. "That just means I'll look young while you're getting all wrinkled and gray."

"Hey." Chase gave Holt a fist bump.

"He's in the back corner scowling." Holt grinned. "I've been keeping an eye on him for ya."

"Thanks." Chase was happy to know the big bouncer was looking out for him. He gestured to Rusty. "Holt, this is my roommate Rusty. He's a bar virgin."

Holt's eyes rounded. "Really?" He took Rusty's driver's license. "Well, welcome to Clean Slate, Icarus Bonham."

Chase's jaw dropped. "Icarus? You're fucking name's Icarus?"

Rusty narrowed his eyes. "Tell anyone, and I'll spill a few of your secrets."

Chase held up his hands. He'd told Rusty a lot of private shit. "I'm not telling anyone, but Icarus? Damn."

"Sorry," Holt told Rusty. "I didn't mean to out you."

Rusty shrugged. "I'm used to it."

Chase took his coat off as he made his way through the crowd. He glanced over his shoulder at Rusty who was barely keeping up. "If we lose each other, I'm headed to the back corner," he yelled over the music.

Rusty nodded. The poor guy looked scared to death. Maybe Chase should have initiated Rusty to the bar scene on a less crowded night. Typical Friday, the place was elbow to elbow with partiers.

Chase spotted Mac. Zeke had been right, the vultures were definitely circling. He watched as Mac shook his head in answer to whatever the hot young co-ed was saying in his ear.

Mac glanced up and met Chase's gaze. As corny as it sounded, the whole crowd seemed to disappear as Chase made his way to Mac's table. "Thanks for waiting," Chase said, dropping his coat over one of the stools.

The co-ed said something in Mac's ear that Chase couldn't hear. "Fuck off," Mac said to the man. When Chase started to sit down, Mac shook his head and crooked his finger. "Come here."

Chase licked his lips, remembering the kiss he and Mac had shared their first night. God, he wanted another. Mac spun his stool to the side and opened his knees, giving Chase a spot to stand. "Hey," Chase said.

Mac reached out and grabbed Chase by the hips before pulling him deeper into the V of his thighs. "I figured you'd be working."

Chase draped his arms over Mac's broad shoulders. "Reid believes that if you make an employee work both Friday and Saturday night, they'll grow to resent it after a while and just start skipping work to party with their friends. My shift is tomorrow."

Mac slid his hands down to rest on Chase's ass as he pulled him even closer.

"How can you work like this?" Rusty asked, making it to the table. "My butt's bruised just by walking through this place." He rubbed his ass.

Chase laughed. He stared into Mac's eyes. "This is my roommate, Rusty. He drove me so I wouldn't have to catch a bus."

Mac released one of Chase's ass cheeks and held out his hand. "I'm Mac. Thanks for bringing Chase."

Rusty shook Mac's hand. "Had I known what I was in for, I'd have called him a cab."

Wyatt appeared out of nowhere. "Oh, you made it." He winked at Chase. "What can I get you?"

Chase glanced at Mac's empty glass. "You want another?"

"That depends on your plans tonight. If I have another, you'll have to drive me home," Mac whispered in Chase's ear.

Holy fuck. "Another Sam Adams, and I think I'll have a glass of red wine," he told Wyatt. He put his lips to Mac's ear. "I'll nurse that the rest of the evening and still be fine to drive you home."

"Ooh, that sounds good. I'll have a wine, too," Rusty replied.

Chase regarded Rusty. "Really? You're gonna drink?"

"I need something to numb the bruises forming on my ass." Rusty sat on the stool across from Mac. "This'll probably be my first and last trip to this place. Might as well make it count for something."

Laughing, Wyatt left and headed toward the bar.

Mac's lips brushed Chase's neck. "I've been thinking about you."

Chase hated to make out in front of Rusty, but he'd waited too damn long to let the moment pass. He pressed himself against Mac's groin, grateful when he rubbed against the erection trapped behind Mac's fly. "All I do is think about you."

Mac's chest vibrated with a deep moan as he squeezed Chase's ass. "Did you take care of that problem you had?"

Chase broke eye contact. "Not yet." He kissed Mac's jaw. "But I will." His body was on fire with need. The uncontrollable desire was like nothing he'd ever felt. Even when he and Benny had first taken their relationship to a physical level, the passion hadn't been anything like what he felt with Mac. Guilt settled into his gut once more.

"Where's the bathroom?" Rusty asked, interrupting Chase's thoughts.

Chase wasn't sure if Rusty really needed to go or merely felt uncomfortable watching Mac grope him. "Down that hall. It's on the left."

"If I'm not back in ten minutes, send a search party." Rusty slid off the stool and began to push his way through the throng of people.

Chase returned his attention to Mac. "Please don't push me away because I haven't talked to Benny yet."

Mac slid one hand up to the back of Chase's neck. "I'm tired of waiting." He pressed his lips against Chase's.

Chase opened his mouth and accepted Mac's tongue with enthusiasm. He tasted beer and whiskey and wondered how much Mac had had to drink before he'd arrived.

Mac reached up and drew one of Chase's arms off his shoulder. He directed Chase's hand to the bulge in his jeans and moaned when Chase applied pressure to Mac's hard cock.

Wyatt whistled as he set glasses on the table. "Well, don't let me interrupt," he quipped.

Chase broke the kiss. "We won't."

Something metallic-sounding slammed on the table. "There's the key to the storage room if you need it," Wyatt said.

Chase glanced at the silver key. He'd never had sex in a bar. Hell, before Mac, he'd never wanted to, but the thought of bending over a box of cocktail napkins while Mac fucked him felt dirty. "Thanks, but we won't need it."

Mac's eyebrows rose.

Chase squeezed Mac's cock. "As much as I want you to fuck me, I won't be your dirty backroom boy."

Mac stared at Chase. "If all I wanted was a dirty backroom boy, I could've had that an hour ago and three times since."

"Are you saying you want to fuck me in the storage room?" Chase asked. The idea didn't completely suck, but he had been hoping for more.

"No. I'm saying you're the only one I want to fuck, and keeping you a secret isn't the way I do things. That's why it's important that you set things right with your boyfriend because I have a feeling once I fuck you, I'll want seconds"—he kissed Chase's neck—"and thirds." He continued to kiss his way to Chase's lips. "Possibly fourths," he said before thrusting his tongue in Chase's mouth.

In an attempt to cool things off, Chase broke away enough to reach for his glass of wine. "Rusty promised to stay for thirty minutes. After he leaves, I'm all yours."

Mac brushed Chase's cheek with his knuckles. "Once we see your friend on his way, I'd like to get outta here too."

Chase nodded. "I'd like that." He leaned in for another kiss.

Rusty returned to the table. "Professor Ryan's over there with Professor Corto Delgado," he announced.

Chase remembered how the two men had helped Rusty after Rusty's parents were killed. "Go say hi."

Rusty pushed his tiny wire-framed glasses up farther on his nose. "I can't do that. I'd make a fool of myself."

"Saying hi?" Chase questioned.

Rusty took a sip of his wine. "I get tongue-tied when I'm around them."

Although Rusty seemed to lack social skills, Chase had never known his roommate to be anything less than articulate. He watched Rusty's gaze stray across the room. "You like them."

Rusty upended his wine glass and drained the contents. "It's a crush, actually, and most of the people in the department have the same crush, so mine isn't special." He slid off the table. "How much do I owe for the drink?"

"Nothing," Mac spoke up. "I'll take care of it."

Rusty nodded. "Thank you." He shrugged into his coat. "Are you going to be okay here?"

Chase grinned when Mac squeezed his butt. "Don't worry. I'm in good hands."

"It was nice to meet you, Mac." With a small wave, Rusty headed toward the front door.

Chase opened his mouth for another of Mac's deep kisses. Although Mac was a masterful kisser, Chase was ready to get the hell out of there and find out what else Mac had mastered.

"You ready?" Mac asked.

"More than," Chase replied. "I need to duck into the restroom first though."

"I'll find Wyatt and pay my tab." Mac ran his palm down Chase's spine. "You'd better grab your coat so no one takes it."

"Good thinking." Chase picked up the heavy black wool coat his mom had given him for Christmas. He draped his bright red scarf around his neck to keep from dropping it. "I'll meet you at the bar when I'm done."

"Sounds good." Mac brushed a hand against Chase's arm before breaking away.

Chase fought his way through the crowd, saying hi to a few of his regular customers. He entered the restroom and quickly took care of his full bladder before heading toward the bar. When he didn't immediately spot Mac, his gut clenched. Shit.

"Zeke? Have you seen Mac?" Chase asked.

Zeke leaned against the bar and spoke in Chase's ear. "That friend of yours was roughed up in the parking lot. Mac was paying his bill when one of the customers came in and reported it." He jerked his head in the direction of the door. "Mac went out to check on him."

"Thanks." Chase pushed his way through the crowd. The thought of someone hurting his timid and bookish roommate made him seethe. What the fuck was wrong with people? He knew for a fact Rusty hadn't started anything. Hell, it had taken two weeks of rooming together before Rusty would even relax around Chase.

Chase noticed a group of people gathered at the edge of the parking lot and took off at a run. "Rusty?"

Swerving around the crowd, Chase came to a screeching halt. Seated on the cold pavement with Professors Adam Ryan and Manuel Corto Delgado kneeling beside him, Rusty held his broken glasses in his hand.

"Fuck!" Chase screamed in frustration. "What happened?" he asked Mac.

Arms crossed over his muscular chest, Mac shook his head. "Typical gay bashing. They always pick on the weaker ones. I called the police."

"Did you see any of the guys who did it?" Chase cursed himself. If he hadn't begged Rusty to go with him to the bar, none of it would've happened.

"They jumped into a dark blue Mustang and took off as soon as Holt rounded the corner. Holt got a partial on the plate, but they had ski masks on, so even if the security camera caught something, it might be hard to prosecute anyone other than the owner of the car." Mac settled his hand on Chase's lower back. "Why don't you see if Rusty needs anything? So far, he isn't talking to anyone."

Chase nodded. He slowly knelt in front of Rusty. "Hey."

Rusty glanced up from his glasses to look at Chase. "I don't have a spare pair," he mumbled.

Chase swallowed around the lump in his throat. "There's one of those glasses in an hour places at the mall. I can take you in the morning."

"But I need to study tonight," Rusty countered, returning his gaze to the broken wire-framed glasses.

Chase noticed the distressed, but caring, expression on the handsome faces of the professors. He was once again reminded of the way Professor Ryan had taken care of Rusty after the deaths of Rusty's parents. Chase reached out and tilted Rusty's chin up. The cut on his cheekbone was still bleeding, so it was hard to tell how deep the wound was. "Do you need to go to the hospital?"

Rusty's eyes filled with tears. "It's been a long time since I've been beaten up. I forgot how much it hurts."

Chase nodded, knowing what it felt like to be at the mercy of someone bigger and stronger. "Yeah, it does," he agreed.

"We should get him to the emergency room," Professor Corto Delgado said.

"What about the police?" Chase asked.

"They're taking their sweet time," Professor Ryan ground out between clenched jaws. "As far as I'm concerned, they can talk to Rusty either tomorrow or at the hospital."

Chase gently took the glasses from Rusty. "Why don't you let the professors take you to get checked out? At the least, I think you might need a stitch or two to close the cut on your cheek. I'll be there as soon as I can."

Rusty stared at Chase. "I'll have a scar like yours."

Chase absently brushed the crescent-shaped scar on his cheekbone. "You're right, you will."

Rusty closed his eyes for several moments. "I wish I could talk to my mom."

Chase's heart nearly broke in two. *Fuck!* What the hell could he say to that? He pulled the scarf from around his neck and used it to dab at the blood dripping down Rusty's face. "You can talk to me."

Rusty glanced up at Professor Ryan before returning his gaze to Chase. "Maybe."

Chase didn't miss the moment that seemed to pass between Rusty and Professor Ryan. He got to his feet and immediately felt Mac press against his back. "Go ahead and take him to the hospital." He held up Rusty's glasses. "I'll keep these for now."

Professor Corto Delgado scooped Rusty off the pavement and into his muscular arms. The police arrived, and Manuel growled low in his throat. Still carrying Rusty, the professor stalked over to the cops and said something Chase couldn't hear. The cop nodded.

"I'll call Charlie and be there as soon as I can," Chase told Professor Ryan before the handsome man rushed off.

"Who's Charlie?" Mac asked.

"Charlie Salinger. He's the director in charge of BK House," Chase answered, turning to wrap his arms around Mac. "This late, Charlie will probably send Locky, the guy in charge of students, to the hospital.

"Sorry." He kissed Mac's jaw. "I know this isn't how you wanted the evening to go."

Mac gave Chase a quick kiss on the lips. "I wanted to spend time with you." He took a deep breath and let it out slowly. "It's hard to keep my hands off you, and I don't think that's gonna change anytime soon."

Chase's body reacted predictably. He pressed his erection against Mac. "Christ! My roommate's just been beaten, and my dick's hard."

Mac chuckled. "I know the feeling." He kissed Chase again, slipping his tongue inside for a brief moment before pulling back. "Let's take care of Rusty before I get carried away and fuck you in the back of my pickup."

Chase grinned. It was twenty-three degrees outside. "I think I'd suffer a cold ass for you."

Mac closed his eyes and shook his head slowly from side to side. "You're trouble."

Chapter Three

Mac waited beside Locky while Chase ducked his head into the backseat of Manuel's sleek sedan. The roommates shared a few words before Chase withdrew from the car.

The moment the three men drove off, Locky turned to Chase. "Is there something going on there?"

Chase shrugged. "I didn't think so, but the way they both insisted on taking Rusty home with them makes me think twice. The fact that Rusty finally agreed nearly floored me."

Mac dug his keys out of his pocket. "You ready?"

Chase glanced up at Mac. "You still want me to go with you? Because Locky can take me back to BK if you're tired."

Mac held out his free hand to shake Locky's. "Thanks for coming, but I'll get Chase home." *Eventually*, he mentally added.

"Okay." Locky squeezed Chase's shoulder. "Rusty's going to be fine after a few days of rest."

"Yeah," Chase agreed. "He made me promise to gather his books and take them over to Professor

Ryan's loft tomorrow." He dug Chase's glasses out of his coat pocket. "I'm going to go by tomorrow morning and see if they can replace the lenses in these and straighten out the frames. Professor Corto Delgado told me to have the store call him for a credit card number over the phone."

Seemingly satisfied, Locky released Chase's shoulder. "It was nice to meet you, Mac. Chase, I'll see you in the morning."

Mac reached for Chase's hand. "Ready?"

Chase smiled up at him. "Hell yeah," he answered, pulling Mac toward the pickup.

Mac felt lighter and younger than he had in years as he followed Chase. Although he still hadn't slept with Chase, he'd thought about him more often than anyone he'd been with since he'd first met his ex-wife. If he were honest, the idea of really liking Chase scared the shit out of him. With casual fucks, there was no need to exchange histories, no need to open up about the mistakes he'd made in his life, but he knew from experience that nothing good could happen without total and complete honesty.

They reached the truck and Mac opened Chase's door. It was a stupid habit he'd picked up in his early life and not every man appreciated the gesture. A broad smile lit up Chase's handsome face, telling Mac otherwise. "Thank you," Chase said before tilting his head back for a kiss.

Mac pulled Chase into his arms and kissed the man hard and deep. He loved the taste of Chase. The moaning sound Chase made when he was revving up, heated Mac's blood and hardened his cock.

Unable to stop himself, Mac reached between them and palmed Chase's erection through the worn denim of his jeans. "Goddamn, you drive me crazy."

Chase pushed his cock against Mac's hand. "I've been hard since the first night I met you."

Mac glanced around, wondering if there were security cameras trained on them. What he wouldn't give to unzip Chase's fly and peel the jeans off the sexy fucker, but the threat of being caught on camera cooled his ardor. He mentally calculated the time it would take for him to get home and silently cursed. "Get in."

Chase climbed up and moved to the center of the bench seat. "This okay?" he asked as Mac slid behind the steering wheel.

Although not totally blacked out, the slight tint of the windows offered a modicum of privacy once Mac shut the door. He started the engine, hoping the heater warmed up faster than it usually did before leaning over to give Chase another deep kiss. He wanted more. *Fuck.* The thought of driving all the way to his house in the country before feeling Chase's hands on his naked body wouldn't do. He thought of the twin bed in the backroom of the shop. He didn't use it often, but on occasion, the weather forced him to stay in town. He wondered if Chase would be turned off by fucking with the lingering smell of gas and motor oil on the sheets. He shook his head. No, it wasn't an option.

"Maybe you'd better put some distance between us," Mac said, breaking the kiss. "My place's about eight miles out of town, and I don't trust myself to get us there in one piece with you so close."

Chase laughed. "I was just wondering if you'd let me give you a hand job on the way to your house."

Mac squeezed the steering wheel in a white-knuckled grip. "If you're trying to tease me, don't. At this point, I'm libel to pull you onto my lap and fuck you right here in the parking lot."

"Shit." Chase's hands dropped to squeeze his own thighs. He closed his eyes and took several deep breaths before reaching over his shoulder for the safety harness. "Drive."

Glad he wasn't the only one hard and wanting, Mac threw the truck into gear. After ten minutes of uncomfortable silence, he decided to get his mind off Chase's body by learning more about him. "So, what're you studying?"

Chase rubbed his hands back and forth on his legs so fast Mac expected to see flames erupt from the denim any moment. "I hope to teach history, and if all goes well, coach football at a junior or senior high somewhere." He continued to stare out the passenger window. "How much farther?"

"We're halfway there," Mac replied.

"As soon as we get out of town, pull over somewhere."

Mac turned his head and met Chase's gaze. "You okay?"

Chase shook his head. "I'm two seconds away from jacking off. I don't know what the hell you're doing to me, but I've never felt this kind of need before."

Fuck. The thought of watching Chase pleasure himself made him groan. "Do it." He slowed his speed when he pulled onto the two-lane highway that led to his house.

"Thank you." Chase unzipped and within seconds had his cock in his hand.

"Hang on." Mac slowed the truck before leaning over to pop open the glove box. The small light inside illuminated Chase's groin perfectly. He'd have rather turned the overhead light on, but decided it would be too risky.

After spitting in his hand, Chase started at the base of his cock and worked his way up. "Oh fuck," he moaned. "God, I thought I was going to explode in my jeans."

Mac tried to keep his eyes on the road while taking quick glances at the sight of Chase working his cock. He reached over and swiped the head of Chase's cock, gathering a good amount of pre-cum on his thumb. When he stuck his thumb in his mouth, the taste of Chase exploded on his tongue. *Shit.*

"Don't come," Mac ordered, taking a sharp right onto a seldom-used gravel road. They were still about four miles from his house, but he couldn't stand the thought of Chase's cum being wasted. He slammed on the brakes and put the truck in park before leaning over to engulf Chase's length.

Chase tore off Mac's beanie and ran his palm over Mac's short hair.

With his mouth full of cock, Mac tensed when Chase's finger followed the long scar on top of his head. He prepared himself for the barrage of questions that was sure to follow, but groaned instead when he felt Chase's soft lips kiss the scar.

"Suck the head. I'm gonna cum," Chase warned, bucking up into Mac's mouth.

Mac pulled back enough to lave the crown as Chase's body tensed.

"Fuck!" Chase howled.

Mac closed his lips around the head of Chase's cock. Strands of cum shot onto the back of his throat as Mac fought to keep his own orgasm at bay. It had been years since he'd sucked someone off, even longer since he'd enjoyed it, but damn, did he love the taste of

Chase's cum. He cleaned Chase's cock before sitting up enough to take Chase's mouth in a deep kiss.

Breaking away, Chase stared at Mac. "You?"

Mac shook his head and reluctantly resumed his seat behind the wheel. "I plan to be buried inside you when I come."

Chase sighed. "I'd love that."

* * * *

Despite the cold, Chase started undressing on the way from the truck to the farmhouse. He loved old places like Mac's but would have to save his adoration until after he'd spent a night fucking.

"What the hell're you doing? You're going to freeze your ass off." Mac ran ahead of Chase onto the deep front porch.

His blood still pumping from his earlier orgasm, Chase didn't worry about his bits suffering frostbite. By the time Mac had the door unlocked, Chase's coat, shirt and sneakers were off and he was working on his jeans.

"Shit," Mac said, grabbing Chase's clothes. He threw them into the house as Chase pushed his jeans and underwear to the small area rug just inside the door.

Naked, Chase turned his attention to Mac. Instead of getting undressed, Mac was leaning against the front door with his hands shoved into his coat pockets.

"What?" Chase asked.

Mac slowly shook his head from side to side. "Your ass is a work of art."

Chase was surprised by the praise. Although not huge, the bubble butt he'd been born with had always bothered him. "I hate my ass. I bought a pair of those super low-rise jeans Wyatt and Zeke wear and had to take them back because half my damn crack was on display."

Mac shrugged out of his coat and let it drop to the floor. "It's pure muscle." He moved to stand next to Chase before cupping the twin globes in his big hands. "Fuck, babe, your body is amazing."

Pleased with the compliment, Chase grabbed the hem of Mac's tight gray shirt. "Take this off. I want to see you."

Releasing Chase's butt, Mac pulled the shirt over his head, knocking his hat off in the process. "Come on." He grabbed Chase's hand and led him up the staircase.

Chase stared at Mac's broad back as they made their way down a short hallway to a bedroom. The room was dark, save for the moonlight shining through the open curtains.

"Lights?" Mac asked, sitting on the side of the bed to pull off his heavy black boots.

Chase stared at the mattress. He'd never had sex in a bed. With three men constantly coming and going from Benny's house and Chase's mother always at home, he and Benny had found other places to have sex, old barns, fields and on more than one occasion, the locker room at the high school.

"Chase?"

Chase blinked. "Yeah, whatever."

Mac took off his jeans before moving to turn on a small lamp in the corner of the room. The low watt bulb bathed everything in a soft amber glow. "That okay?"

His nerves starting to kick in, Chase simply nodded. He didn't budge from his spot just inside the door until Mac pulled back the blankets on the bed.

"You coming?" Mac asked, withdrawing a strip of condoms and lube from the nightstand.

"Yeah." Chase slid into bed. He tried to push thoughts of Benny out of his mind. It wasn't the first time he'd had sex with someone other than Benny, and he'd been upfront with Benny when it came to him seeing other people while they were separated, so why did he feel guilty?

The answer came to Chase as soon as Mac pulled him into his arms. Mac was different from the guys he'd let fuck him in the past because with Mac, it didn't feel like a one-night stand. He opened his mouth when Mac kissed him and thoughts of Benny drifted away, leaving only the desire for the man holding him.

Mac continued to probe Chase's mouth with his tongue as his hand ventured south to Chase's cock.

Chase draped his leg over Mac's hip, his cock hardening despite coming less than fifteen minutes earlier. Never had a man turned him on like Mac. What was it about Mac that had him determined to break the heart of the sweetest man he'd ever known?

Mac's hand released Chase's cock. He broke the kiss long enough to say, "I love this ass."

The brush of Mac's finger against his hole made Chase jerk with need. *Fuck.* He'd spent too many nights wondering what it would be like to have Mac inside him, and while the touch was welcome, it wasn't enough. He needed more. He wanted everything Mac had to give.

Breaking the kiss, Mac reached behind him and grabbed the bottle of lube. "I need to feel you," he said, his voice gruff.

Chase started to move, but Mac held him in place with the arm under Chase's torso.

"Stay right there." Mac handed Chase the bottle before holding out his hand. "Drip some of that onto my fingers."

Chase did as asked. He wasn't sure what to do with the bottle once he'd accomplished the task and ended up pushing it between them until he could roll away far enough to set it back on the table.

Mac's slick fingers began to circle and dip into Chase's hole. "I'd have compromised my stance on your boyfriend back home earlier if I'd known you'd feel so good in my bed."

Although incredibly flattered by the statement, it reminded Chase of what he still needed to do. It wasn't burgeoning love that cemented his decision to talk to Benny, it was the way Mac made him feel with such a simple touch. Sex with Benny had been nice and sweet, like Benny, but never before had his body vibrated with need like it did with Mac.

"As much as I want to lick every inch of you, I need to fuck you first," Mac growled, inserting his middle finger to the hilt.

"God, yes," Chase agreed. He moaned when another finger slid into him. "Will you fuck me from behind?"

Mac's fingers slowed. "Is that what you want?"

Chase bit his bottom lip. Benny had always made love to him face to face, but the few men he'd been with outside of Cattle Valley always took him from behind. He didn't know which he preferred. From behind seemed too casual while missionary was too intimate. "I don't know. What do you think?"

Mac answered by rolling to his back and reaching for a condom.

It was Chase's first real glimpse of Mac's erection and tattooed chest. He didn't know what to examine first. Mac's cock was impressive, probably the biggest he'd ever seen, but Chase's gaze strayed to the impressive tattoo that covered Mac's shoulder. Although not apparent on first glance, there were bumps and ridges in the tattoo. He drew his finger along a series of scars that ran like tree branches on Mac's skin.

Mac grabbed Chase's hand, stilling it. "Don't," he snapped.

The gruff command reminded Chase of his father. "Sorry," he mumbled, pulling his hand free. He sat up, prepared to ask Mac to take him back to the dorm.

"Hey." Mac wrapped his arms around Chase's waist. "I'm sorry." When Chase didn't say anything, Mac cursed. "Fuck." He sighed and rested his cheek on Chase's thigh. "I can't talk about the scars without telling you about the worst parts of who I used to be. I wanted to give this thing between us a chance before I scared you away."

Chase's hand hovered over Mac's head for several moments before finally giving into the need to touch him. He wasn't sure he could deal with not knowing. "I only have one question. Did you beat your son or ex-wife?"

Mac sprang up to a seated position. "What?"

Chase knew he couldn't question Mac further without revealing his biggest fears. He stared at Mac, praying the man was worth the pain it would cause to venture back to the past, even if only in his mind. "My dad hit us. I need to know if you're like him, and if that's the reason your son won't talk to you."

Drawing Chase close, Mac shook his head. "God, no." He kissed Chase's temple. "Jackson won't see me or talk to me because I'm gay." He kissed Chase again. "I'm sorry your dad hurt you."

Chase relaxed and allowed Mac to ease him down to the mattress.

"I'm not ready to go into detail about what happened in my marriage, but you have to believe me when I say I'd never raise a hand to you." Mac seemed to curl himself around Chase, peppering Chase's face and neck with kisses. "I know I come off as a rough bastard sometimes, but I love my son more than my own life."

Chase couldn't understand why Mac's son had reacted the way he had, but he felt better knowing it wasn't for the reason he'd been afraid of. He wrapped his arms around Mac. "I had to make sure." He hoped Mac understood.

Mac pulled back enough to stare into Chase's eyes and nodded. "Skeet's dad liked to rough him up when we were kids. I know what that does to a person. As uncomfortable as it was to be accused of something like that, I understand."

"Thanks," Chase mumbled.

"I take it he's the reason you shy away from confrontation." Mac's hands rubbed up and down Chase's back in a soothing gesture.

Chase closed his eyes. He hated to talk about his father, detested the way it made him feel, but he'd brought it up, so he felt he owed Mac an explanation. "I used to get in a lot of trouble when I was young. I still don't know whether I was a bad kid or if my dad just didn't like me, but he was always yelling. When my mom tried to step in, he would take it out on her."

"How'd you and your mom get away from him?" Mac asked.

Chase drew Mac's attention to the crescent-shaped scar on his cheekbone. "I got this because I got sacked twice in a Pop Warner game. When we got home, my dad said I was pathetic and needed to toughen up." He sighed. "He hit me with his fist, and my mom heard me cry out. She came into the room and got between us. That's when he started on her." Chase shook his head. "It was worse than ever, and I thought he was going to kill her, so I ran into the kitchen and called the police."

Mac kissed Chase's forehead.

"Mom and I got stitched up and left while the police still had dad in custody." Chase shrugged. "Mom had a friend from work who'd moved to Cattle Valley a couple years earlier, so that's where we went. I don't think mom cared where we ended up as long as we were safe. Dad would've never looked for us in a town full of gays, he hated gays." He looked up at Mac. "I think that's why he always hated me. I didn't know I was gay back then, but maybe he did."

Mac's finger traced Chase's scar for several heartbeats. "You were a boy. You can't let your father's actions follow you for the rest of your life. Saying that, there's nothing wrong with avoiding confrontation as long as you don't compromise who you are in the process." He leaned in and gave Chase a deep kiss before pulling back. "I like you a lot, but I can't worry every time I raise my voice that you're gonna back away. I'm a moody sonofabitch at times, but I'll never lay a hand on you out of anger."

Staring at Mac, Chase knew what he had to do. He had no idea where things would go with Mac or if they'd go anywhere, but he knew putting off the talk with Benny was definitely compromising the man he wanted to be. "I'm off on Sunday and have a light class load on Monday. I'm going to take the bus home and have the conversation with Benny that I've put off for too long."

Mac rolled on top of Chase. "You don't have to do that because of me. I won't push you. Not knowing what I do now."

Chase wrapped his legs around Mac's waist. "I like you a lot, too, but I'm not doing it for you. It's time I get over myself and face the situation between me and Benny head on."

Mac rubbed his hardening cock against Chase. "I can take a couple days off if you want me to take you home."

Chase shook his head. "As much as I'd enjoy spending the time with you, I can't do that to Benny. I'll be honest with him, and I'm sure you'll come up in the conversation, but it would hurt him even more if he knew you'd brought me."

Mac buried his face against Chase's neck. "Okay," he whispered, kissing Chase's neck. "But you're taking my truck. No bus."

Chase started to decline the offer, but Mac took his mouth in a deep kiss. Chase wound his arms around Mac's neck and poured everything he had into the kiss. The chemistry that had been between them since their first meeting ignited. His hands wandered down Mac's back to land on his muscled ass. "Fuck me," he said, breaking the kiss for air.

"Are you sure? It's been a rough night for you."

Chase grinned. Despite the passion that blazed between them, the hard-edged biker still cared enough to ask. In that moment, he knew Mac was absolutely nothing like his father, and he wanted to feel Mac inside him. "Positive."

Mac sheathed his cock before looking around. "What happened to the lube?"

Chase sat up. "I think it's been stabbing me in the back." He turned and grabbed the bottle. After flicking open the lid, he dripped lube down Mac's hard length. "Impressive," he said, sliding his hand up and down Mac's cock.

Mac brushed his fingers over Chase's cock. "I could say the same." He rested his head on his free hand and smiled. "Wanna ride?"

Chase released Mac's cock and used the excess lube on his hand to reach behind himself and make sure he was stretched enough to accommodate Mac's girth. He moaned when he rocked back and forth on his own fingers.

"Shit." Mac thrust his hips toward Chase. "Climb on."

Chase withdrew his fingers and moved to straddle Mac's hips. His first instinct was to slam his ass down on Mac's cock, but he decided against it when he felt the initial stretch as Mac's crown breached his hole. Benny's cock was long and Chase had always assumed it was thicker than most, but Mac was even bigger.

Mac hissed as Chase slowly lowered himself. "Goddamn, you're tight."

Other than a slight burn, Chase's body accepted Mac's entire length without a lot of pain. He settled his ass against Mac and sighed. "You feel good."

Mac wrapped one arm around Chase and pulled him down for a kiss. The movement eased a few inches of Mac's cock out of Chase's ass, but before Chase could complain, Mac thrust his hips and filled Chase once more. "Let me hold you while I fuck you," Mac said.

Chase let his feet slide down the mattress until his knees took their place on either side of Mac's groin. "I'd like that."

Mac grabbed Chase's ass and thrust his hips.

It took several heartbeats, but eventually Chase caught Mac's rhythm. He began to move in counterpoint to Mac's thrusts, driving Mac's cock deep. It wasn't until he realized he and Mac were staring at each other that he knew he could have the talk with Benny without the guilt that had plagued him for months. It wasn't love he saw in Mac's gaze. It was far too soon for an emotional connection between them, but in Mac's eyes, Chase saw the potential for something real. He'd had the emotional connection with Benny without the physical desire and knew for a fact that he needed both to be happy. He also knew Benny deserved the same thing, and with Benny's big heart and gorgeous body, his first love would find it.

Suddenly, Mac rolled them, putting Chase underneath him. He hooked Chase's knees with his arms, spreading Chase's legs open, wide enough for him to fit between them. "It's been a long time since I've felt this good," he panted between thrusts.

Chase accepted the compliment but found it hard to believe. "With the way you look, I'd expect you to have someone different in this bed every night."

Mac thrust deep and stilled.

Chase couldn't read the expression on Mac's face and started to worry that he'd said something wrong. "I'm sorry."

Mac shook his head. "I had a brief relationship a couple years ago, but other than that, you're the first I've brought home."

Chase wasn't sure what to say. He hadn't been pulling Mac's chain when he'd complimented his looks. Mac was the sexy tattooed biker-type that a lot of men and women were into lately. It wasn't necessarily the biker-style, it was Mac's tall, muscular frame and the tattoos that Chase had first noticed. He wiggled his ass in an attempt to get Mac moving again. That expression was still on Mac's face, and Chase didn't know what else to do or say. "I'm glad you brought me home with you," he finally replied.

"I'll be thirty-five in April," Mac said.

"Okay." Chase ran his hands down Mac's spine. "I'll remember that."

Mac shook his head. "I'm a lot older than you are."

Chase thought of the couples back in Cattle Valley that were together and going strong despite their age differences. "That doesn't bother me. As long as you aren't embarrassed by the fact that I'm younger, I don't see a problem."

Mac withdrew his cock before surging deep. "I'm far from being embarrassed, QB."

It was Chase's turn to shake his head. "Please don't call me that."

Mac's eyes rounded as he began to fuck Chase again. "I thought that's what everyone at the bar called you."

"It is, but that's because that's all I am to them." Chase licked his lips. "But to you, I wanna be more than the position I play."

Mac released his hold on Chase's legs and stretched out on top of him, putting them nose to nose. "I wanted you before I even knew your name, so you're a lot more to me than the position you play."

Chase opened his mouth when Mac pressed their lips together. He rubbed his tongue against Mac's as he wrapped his legs around Mac's waist. With Mac's body on top of him, rubbing against the length of his cock, each thrust of Mac's hips sent tingles throughout Chase's body. He broke the kiss. "I'm gonna come."

Mac nodded twice. "It's about time. I've been holding on by a thread for the last five minutes."

Chase chuckled. "Come with me then. Let's fall together."

Mac's expression sobered once again. "Yeah."

Chase came three thrusts later, shooting between them. He was surprised at the intensity of his orgasm after having filled Mac's mouth earlier and held onto Mac with all the strength he had left.

"Oh, fuck, babe!" Mac cried out as he buried his cock to the hilt and followed Chase over the edge. He rested his forehead against Chase's as his body began to relax. "Shit," he groaned, closing his eyes.

"Babe's good," Chase said on a sigh. "I can deal with that one."

* * * *

Mac wiped the sleep from his eyes as he transferred bacon to two plates. "Eggs?"

Chase glanced up from his phone. "Sure. Three hard, please."

Mac retrieved the carton from the refrigerator. He'd picked Chase up from his shift the previous night and had taken him to BK house to pack a suitcase before bringing him home. Once again, the two of them had spent the entire night fucking. Napping only long enough to recharge before going at it again. "How long's your drive?" It was hard for him to make small talk when all he could think about was sex with Chase. He'd started having sex at the age of thirteen and couldn't count the number of bed partners he'd enjoyed over the years, both men and women, but even as jaded as he'd become after his divorce, he knew he and Chase were good together. Unfortunately, he also knew how hard it would be to see Chase walk away when the newness of the situation wore off.

"A little over twelve hours." Chase bit his bottom lip as he stared at the text that had just come through. "I'm hoping to talk to Benny tonight. He's got school tomorrow, so if I don't do it tonight, I won't get back until Tuesday at the earliest."

Mac flipped the bacon grease over the eggs. He didn't mind getting Skeet to pick him up from work Tuesday as well, but he didn't like Chase making such a long trip on his own. He understood why it wasn't a good idea for him to tag along, but twelve hours was a long stretch to drive alone. "What if I help you with the drive and stay at a hotel outside of town? No one but you would even have to know I made the trip."

"You really don't have to do that," Chase argued. "I'm used to taking the bus, and it takes a hell of a lot longer that way."

"I haven't taken time off since I opened the shop. It's not going to hurt to close up for a few days." Mac transferred the eggs from the frying pan to the plates. He set Chase's breakfast in front of him. "Besides, a couple of days out of town sounds pretty damn good. The longer winter goes on, the more I get sick of looking at the same scenery all the time."

Chase took a sip of his orange juice. "Well, if you're sure, I'd like that." He took a bite of his eggs. "I can't say I'll be good company on the way home though. I'm scared shitless about talking to Benny, so I'll probably be wired until I get it over with. Afterwards though..." he trailed off and shrugged.

Mac knew exactly what Chase was faced with. He'd tried to figure out a way to tell Janice he was tired of living a lie for almost two years. Then he'd almost died and realized life was too damn short to be anything but what he truly was. He reached across the table and squeezed Chase's hand. "We'll get you through it."

Chapter Four

Mac turned up the old Lynyrd Skynyrd song and grinned when Chase started pumping his fist into the air and singing at the top of his lungs. "Now I know for a fact you weren't even born when this song was popular."

Chase stopped singing long enough to flash his brilliant smile. "It's a classic. Besides, my mom listens to all this old stuff."

Mac rolled his eyes. Although the song was recorded in seventy-four and he wasn't born until seventy-nine, he wasn't sure he liked being lumped into the oldies class. They were seven hours into the drive, and he'd enjoyed every minute of it.

"Sweet home Alabama," Chase sang as he did a little dance in the seat. He pointed his finger at Mac. "Come on, sing with me."

Shaking his head, Mac refused. His deep voice didn't lend itself well to most songs, and unless there was a Barry White song on the radio, he kept his singing to the shower. "I'd rather hear you," he replied. Chase wasn't a very good singer either, but what he lacked in vocal ability, he more than made up for in enthusiasm. It was damn cute, and Mac had to grip the steering wheel tighter to keep from reaching out to his songbird.

When the song ended, Chase reached over and turned the radio down. "That was fun."

"Yeah, it was," Mac agreed. He glanced at the textbooks in the seat between them. "You get your homework done?"

Chase dug out a bag of Cheetos from their road-food sack. "Pretty much. I'll have to study some more for the test before I get back, but we can do that on the way home."

For two hours, Mac had quizzed Chase on the Korean War and was pleasantly surprised when Chase went beyond the questions to tell Mac stories of individual events. One thing was for sure, Chase was a hell of a lot better student than Mac had ever been. Although, to give himself some credit, he bet Chase hadn't learned how to rebuild an engine by the age of eleven.

Mac glanced over at Chase, who was munching away. He reached out and grabbed Chase's wrist before pulling the hand that held three Cheetos to his mouth. After eating the crunchy twists, he took the time to lick the orange from Chase's fingers.

Chase moaned. "You'd better stop that. I've been good this whole trip except for that bj in the bathroom a few hours ago."

It was Mac's turn to groan. Just thinking about the blowjob Chase had given him was enough to get his dick hard again. He released Chase's wrist. They were on a tight schedule if they wanted to reach Cattle Valley before Benny went to bed for the night. No way did they have time to stop every couple of hours to play. He adjusted his cock. "You're right. You'd better stay over on your side."

Chase laughed. "I've been on my side. I can't help it if you can't keep your hands off this fine body I'm rockin'." He ran his hands down his torso, leaving a few light orange streaks on his white T-shirt. "Shit," he said, noticing what he'd done. He tried to brush off the stains but eventually gave up and shrugged.

That was Chase in a nutshell. Mac liked the fact that Chase didn't take himself too seriously or make a big deal out of shit that didn't really matter. He wished Chase would spend the night with him in the hotel, but Chase worried that his mother would be upset if he didn't stay with her. Mac understood, but he didn't have to like it.

* * * *

"Record time," Chase said, pointing to the clock on the radio when they drove into Sheridan, Wyoming.

Mac started looking for a hotel close to the highway Chase would have to take to Cattle Valley. "What time do you think you'll be back in the morning?"

"Early. Hopefully I'll catch you still in bed." Chase started to clean up the snacks that had spilled from the sack of junk food.

"Tell me what time, and I'll make sure I'm still in bed," Mac replied.

"Five? That'll mean I have to leave home at four, but after talking to Benny, I probably won't sleep much anyway." Chase worried his bottom lip with his teeth. "I still haven't figured out what to say to him."

"Does he know you're coming?" Mac asked, pulling into a hotel parking lot. The hotel sat next to a small diner that looked perfect for a late dinner and early morning breakfast before they would hit the road.

"Yeah. I called him yesterday after you dropped me off at BK. I told him I needed to talk to him and that I was driving over." Chase sighed. "I think he knows. He said something about me being distant lately, and that he was having a hard time with it."

Mac parked under the hotel awning at the front entrance. For the last few hours, he'd struggled with what to say to Chase once they arrived. He wasn't the kind of man to make promises just to make someone feel better. He had no idea where his relationship with Chase was going, but he knew he wanted to find out. Still, he didn't want Chase to regret breaking things off with Benny if things between them didn't work out. "You don't have to do this on my account."

Chase unbuckled before sliding across the bench seat. "I like you," he said. "But, I think I'm doing this more for Benny than anyone else. It's gonna break his heart, and he'll probably hate me or punch me before the night's over, but it's the right thing to do."

Mac leaned down and gave Chase a deep kiss. "I'll have my phone on in case you want to call later."

"I'll either call or text." Chase shrugged. "Depends on how bad it is."

Mac wished he could protect Chase from the coming conversation, but he was proud of him for finally doing it. "I'm here if and when you need me." He wanted to pull Chase into his arms and carry him to the hotel room, but kept his hands in his lap. "Let me get a room before you leave. I'll get two keys, so you can sneak in and crawl into bed with me in the morning."

"Okay." Chase's good-natured mood that had lasted the entire trip was gone.

* * * *

After stopping by home to change his shirt and give his mom a kiss, Chase parked in front of Benny's house. He groaned when he saw three vehicles already parked in the driveway. It was bad enough that Benny's dad, Brian, was home, but Brian's partners, Pete and Ethan seemed to be in residence as well.

Chase was saved when Benny immediately walked out the front door and toward the truck. Fuck. Fuck. Fuck. He tried to slow his racing heart.

Benny opened the passenger door. "Whose truck?"

"A friend's," Chase replied.

Benny got in but made no move to scoot closer to Chase. "What friend?"

Chase swallowed around the lump in his throat. Telling Benny about Mac wouldn't do them any good. "Just a friend," he answered. "You wanna go to the park?"

Benny shook his head and fisted his hands in his lap. "If you're going to break up with me, I'd rather you just got it over with."

"I love you, you know I do, but I'm…"

"Fucking other guys?" Benny asked, cutting Chase off.

Chase unbuckled his seat belt and turned in the seat to face Benny. "I don't love you like you deserve to be loved. You were my first, and you'll always hold a special place in my heart, but I can't do this anymore. I told you I was going to see other people at school, and you agreed, and I can't help but think if we were both truly in love with each other, that wouldn't have happened."

"I do love you," Benny mumbled, finally looking up to meet Chase's gaze. "You're the only person I think about. I knew I couldn't tell you no and still keep you."

Chase felt the burn of tears as he continued to stare at Benny. He wanted to tell Benny how quickly he was going to catch someone's attention once he got to college but knew it wasn't the time. "I haven't been a good boyfriend for a while now, and you deserve so much more than I can give you."

"Save it." Benny licked his lips. "My dad tried to tell me that we wouldn't last, but I refused to listen."

"I've changed. College is a whole different world, you'll see. By this time next year, you won't be the same person either." Chase knew he was fucking it up, but he couldn't stand the broken expression on Benny's handsome face. "I'll understand if you decide to go somewhere else to school, but I hope you don't because you're still one of my best friends."

Benny shook his head. "Seeing you around campus with other guys? I don't know how I'm going to handle that, but the football scholarships have all been given out already, so the only other choice I have is to not play."

"You don't have to worry about that. I'm on campus only long enough to go to class or hit the football field." Chase doubted he was making Benny feel better, but he had to try. Football was Benny's life, and the thought of Benny giving up the scholarship sat like a heavy rock in Chase's gut.

Benny turned his attention to a cat walking across the street. "I can't believe this is happening." He hit the passenger window with his elbow in frustration.

The glass rattled and Chase couldn't believe the damn thing hadn't broken. He moved closer to the driver's door even though he knew in his heart Benny would never hit him. "I'm sorry, but I can't help the way I feel. I've been fighting with it for a while."

Benny narrowed his eyes. "I fucked you at Christmas, and you didn't say a goddamn thing. How could you do that to me?"

Chase wiped at the tears that had escaped. "Despite what you think, I do still love you, just not the way I should. The last thing I wanted was to hurt you, but I realized I was hurting you more by not being honest."

Benny sat, staring out of the passenger window for several minutes. Finally, Benny brushed the tears from his own cheeks and opened the door. "Don't call me. Don't text me," he said before climbing out. He slammed the door shut without meeting Chase's gaze and stalked toward the house.

Chase blew out a ragged breath. His hands were shaking so badly that he could barely turn the key, but he knew he didn't want to be sitting outside Benny's house once Benny told the rest of his family.

Chase drove around the block and parked. He rested his forehead on the steering wheel and took several deep breaths, trying to calm his racing heart. He doubted he'd ever forget the hurt he'd seen in Benny's eyes. It was the first time he'd broken someone's heart, and he decided right then and there he didn't like having that kind of power.

Mac. Chase groaned. Mac didn't seem like the type who would fall in love quickly, but Chase needed to make sure of his feelings before spending too much time with the tattooed hunk.

* * * *

Chase dropped Mac's keys in the bowl just inside the front door. It was late and he doubted his mom was still up, so he quietly made his way to the kitchen.

Gwen Hughes glanced up from the book she was reading when Chase entered the kitchen. "You okay?"

Chase shook his head and took the lid off the cookie jar. He retrieved a handful of homemade chocolate chip cookies. He'd told his mom before he'd left for Benny's what he had to do.

Gwen rose and opened the cupboard. She removed a glass before pulling the jug of milk from the refrigerator. "Do you want to talk about it?"

Chase dropped into his usual seat at the table. "I know I did the right thing, but I really hurt him, Mom."

Gwen set the glass of milk in front of Chase. "Broken hearts are a part of growing up. I'm sure that's Benny's first of many." She resumed her seat and closed her book.

"Why haven't you dated anyone since you left Dad?" Chase asked. He'd always wondered and had assumed it had something to do with the lack of available straight men in Cattle Valley, but he'd never asked.

Gwen wrapped a finger around a thick strand of her light brown hair. "I don't know. I've thought about it from time to time, but I don't think I have the ability to trust someone again." She bit her bottom lip. "Without trust, you can't have anything real, so I decided to live my life surrounded by friends instead."

"But you trust your friends," Chase pointed out.

"Yes, but it's different. I love my friends, but my heart isn't as invested as it needs to be with a significant other."

Chase took a bit of one of the cookies. "Yeah, I get that. I haven't had my heart broken yet, but I can tell you it sucks to be the one doing the breaking. I don't think I can do that again."

Gwen placed a hand on Chase's arm. "You're too young to feel that way." She sighed. "Part of living is falling in and out of love. I don't want you to be afraid of giving your heart to someone simply because your old mom is. What I went through with Jimmy was different, and it's something I hope you never have to go through."

Chase took another bite and washed it down with a drink of milk.

"Now, tell me whose truck you're driving?" Gwen asked, a knowing expression on her pretty face.

"It belongs to my friend Mac. He drove over with me and is staying in Sheridan while I'm here," Chase confessed.

"Is this Mac just a friend?"

Chase shook his head. He was thankful he'd always had his mom's full support. Unlike a lot of kids he'd grown up with, Chase had never shied away from talking to his mom. "I really like him, but after tonight I'm not sure if I should."

"Because you're afraid of getting hurt?" Gwen asked.

"Yeah." Chase picked up another cookie and stared at it. "He's a little older than I am, but that's not what worries me."

"What is it then?"

Chase dropped the cookie back to the table. "I've only known him a few weeks, and I think I like him too much. He's so easy to be around, and he makes me feel good about myself."

"And the problem is?" Gwen prompted when Chase didn't continue.

"Older guys tend to look at younger guys as playthings and that's the last thing I want to be." Chase drew his fingers through his hair in frustration. "One minute I don't wanna let him get too close because I'm afraid of getting hurt and the next I'm worried he won't get close enough and just walk away."

Gwen's hand went to her mouth to try to hide her giggle. "I'm happy to see you're normal despite everything you've been through."

"Normal?" Chase questioned and clutched his hands to his chest. "You've always said I was special."

Gwen playfully slapped Chase's arms. "You are special. However, it's normal for even special people to be afraid to put their hearts out there. I don't want you to never fall in love because you're afraid of what might happen. Love is everything when shared with the right person."

Chase felt a wrenching in his heart at the wistful sound of his mom's voice. It wasn't fair that she'd fallen in love with an asshole. He hated that his dad had ruined his mom for other men, for a life she deserved to have. *Fuck.* He was more confused than ever.

"I'm thinking about just heading back to Sheridan tonight. If I want to make class Tuesday morning, we're going to have to leave early." Chase got to his feet. He kissed his mom on the cheek, hating to leave her so soon. "Love you."

"Are you sure you're okay to drive?" Gwen asked, standing to face Chase.

Chase held up the two cookies he still hadn't eaten. "I'll be fine." He stared at his mom. "Are you happy?"

Gwen's eyes rounded in surprise. "Happy?" She shrugged. "I guess so. I'm safe. I have good friends" — she gave Chase a quick kiss—"and the best son a mother could ask for."

Chase's cell phone rang, breaking the tender moment. It was late, so the caller had to be either Mac or Benny. He pulled the phone out of his pocket and looked at the display. "Mr Allenbrand," he informed his mom. "He's probably calling to chew me out."

"You don't have to answer it," Gwen told him.

"Yes. I do." Chase took a deep breath. "Hi, Mr Allenbrand."

"Chase," Brian greeted. "I ought to kick your ass for hurting Benny, but I respect you for doing it in person. I tried to tell him when you left that people change once they leave home."

"I'm sorry. I didn't want to hurt him. I still care a great deal for him, but..."

"You're not in love with him," Brian finished for Chase.

"Yeah."

Brian sighed. "Benny stormed out of the house a few minutes ago. I don't know where he's going but short of forcibly retaining him, we couldn't stop him."

Shit. Benny was six-foot-five of solid muscle. "Thanks for letting me know."

"If he shows up, give me a call," Brian said.

"I will." Chase swallowed around the lump in his throat. Brian was a good man who was worried about his son, but he'd been nothing but kind to Chase. "I really am sorry that I hurt him."

"It was bound to happen. Very few high school romances last. You're a good kid, Chase, but it might be better if you made yourself scarce for a while. At least until we can get Benny over this rough patch."

"I wasn't planning to come back for Spring Break anyway. I need to work. Would it be okay if I called you in a week or so to see how he's doing?" From outside, Chase heard a loud crash and the sound of breaking glass. "Shit. I think Benny's here, and if I'm not mistaken, he just trashed my friend's truck."

"We'll be right there," Brian said before hanging up.

Chase ended the call and handed his mom his phone. He strode to the living room and opened the front door. Christ. A bat-wielding Benny had busted out the windshield of Mac's truck as well as the front two headlights. "Do me a favor and call Mac. Tell him what's happened and ask him if he wants to press charges against Benny." He thought of the minimal amount of money in his savings account. It was his savings for next semester, but the damage was his fault. "Tell him I'll pay for the damage."

Gwen nodded. "I don't think you should go out there."

"I have to. It's my mess." Chase closed the front door behind him. "Benny?"

Benny swung the bat, putting a dent in the driver's door.

"Benny!" Chase screamed, stepping off the porch. "Stop it!"

Benny turned to face Chase. "I know this truck belongs to whoever's fucking you."

Chase wouldn't deny the accusation, he cared too much for Benny to lie to him. "None of this is Mac's fault. It's mine. If you want to hit something, hit me."

Benny dropped the bat and charged at Chase.

Chase's breath left his lungs when he was tackled to the frozen ground. Pinned, he stared up at Benny. "I'm sorry." Fear overwhelmed him, and he felt tears fill his eyes. It was the first time Benny had used his larger size against him. The thought of Benny hitting him broke his heart, even if he deserved it.

Benny's eyes narrowed. "I trusted you. I gave you everything."

"I know," Chase admitted.

"I love you," Benny mumbled.

Chase closed his eyes. "I love you, too, but I'm not in love with you, not anymore. I tried so hard to hang onto my feelings, but I couldn't." He braced himself. "If you need to beat the shit out of me to make yourself feel better, do it."

Instead of Benny's fist smashing into his face, Chase felt soft lips brush across his own before the bulk that had pinned him down released him. He opened his eyes.

Benny was sitting beside Chase, his head down, clenching and unclenching his hands. "I'm so angry, and I don't know what to do about it." He looked at Mac's truck. "Shit."

Chase sat up. He was shaking so badly his teeth chattered. He wasn't sure if it was the cold night air on his skin or the onslaught of fear that had assaulted him moments earlier. "You'll always be special to me, Benny, but I couldn't lie to you anymore." He knew he'd said something similar in the truck, but he needed to make Benny understand. "We were friends before we became lovers, and in my heart, we're still friends."

Benny glanced at Chase. "I don't think I can be friends."

Chase nodded just as Brian's cruiser pulled up. The front door opened, and Chase's mom came out of the house. Like Chase, Gwen didn't handle confrontations well, so it hadn't surprised Chase that she'd stayed in the house until Brian showed up.

Gwen held out Chase's phone. "He'd like to speak to you."

Chase got to his feet and took the phone. "Hey."

"You okay?" Mac asked.

"Not really, but I will be." Chase watched as Pete and Ethan circled the pickup, taking in the damage, as Brian spoke quietly to Benny. "Did Mom tell you about the truck?"

"Yeah. How bad is it?"

"Pretty bad. I don't know what your insurance deductible is, but I'll pay for it." Chase accepted the coat from his mom and shrugged into it. "I have to be honest, you have every right to press charges against Benny, but I'd rather you didn't. He's eighteen now, so it'll kill his scholarship and go on his permanent record."

"Like I told your mom, I'm not going to press charges. Gwen said Benny's dad was there and he's a cop. Can you ask him if he needs to speak to me?"

"Brian's busy with Benny, but Pete's here and he's a deputy, too." Chase walked over to the handsome man. "The owner of the truck would like to talk to you."

Pete took the phone and walked away.

Chase couldn't believe how much damage had been done to the truck in such a short amount of time. It would take at least a day, maybe two, just to get the glass replaced.

Pete stepped in front of Chase and handed him back the phone. "I'll call Gill in the morning. Your friend seems more worried about you than his truck. He wants you to call him after we get Benny out of here. He plans to rent a car and drive down from Sheridan since Gill will probably need to discuss the repairs with him."

Chase nodded, wondering if Mac would stay with him and his mom in their tiny two-bedroom house. The thought of sleeping with Mac in his small double bed with his mom in the next room wouldn't work.

"I'm sorry about the truck," Benny said as he passed by Chase on the way to Brian's car. Ethan got behind the wheel of Benny's car and pulled out first.

Brian stopped in front of Chase. "Thank you for convincing your friend not to press charges." He glanced at Benny over his shoulder. "Pete's going to work with your friend to take care of the insurance deductible." He stuck out his hand. "Benny'll be in school tomorrow. I'd appreciate it if you'd do me a favor and make sure he doesn't see either of you while you're in town."

"Of course," Chase agreed. He watched Brian walk to his car.

"Come on, let's get out of the cold," Gwen said, leading Chase inside.

Chase stood in the living room. "Can I borrow your car? I can drop Mac off at a car rental place and be back here before you have to go to work in the morning."

"You're going to drive to Sheridan tonight?" Gwen shook her head. "You've been on the road all day, and with what just happened you have to be exhausted."

"Maybe it's adrenaline, but I'm wide awake." Chase wasn't sure how to make his mom understand. "According to Pete, Mac's worried about me. I need to show him I'm okay, and I need him to hold me." He held his breath. Although his mom knew he and Benny fooled around, it was the first time he'd talked about anything intimate with her.

Gwen stared at Chase for several moments before retrieving her keys from the green bowl. "Be careful. If you're going to be in town tomorrow, I'll take the day off, so just give me a call when you wake up."

Chase gave his mom a kiss on the cheek. "Thanks. Love you."

"Love you." Gwen shook her head and crossed her arms. "Mac seems nice, by the way."

"He is." Chase ran to his room and grabbed his suitcase. "I'll call ya."

Chapter Five

Mac heard the hotel room door open. He reached over and turned on the bedside lamp. "I was starting to worry."

Chase dropped his suitcase before turning to lock the door. "My phone died, and I left the charger in the truck." He pulled off his running shoes. "Are you mad at me?"

Stretched out on his back, Mac rested his clasped hands behind his head. "I hate that my truck got trashed, but I'm not mad about it." He patted the bed beside him. "Let's get some sleep."

Chase groaned. "I'm going to jump into the shower first, but you don't need to wait up for me." He rubbed his hands over his face. "I just want this day to be over."

Mac watched Chase disappear into the bathroom before turning off the light. He longed to step into the shower with the younger man and help him forget all about the previous few hours, but Chase had made it clear he wanted to be alone. He couldn't blame Chase.

It had taken him years to gather the courage to break things off with Janice. Years of pretending to be what he wasn't, of longing to be held by masculine arms instead of the thin, fine-boned arms of his wife. He huffed out a breath and rolled to his side.

When he'd received the call from Gwen, it had taken all his strength to do the right thing and let Chase handle the situation. His initial instinct was to make Benny pay for hurting Chase. The truck could be fixed, but he knew firsthand what words spoken in anger could do to a person.

It was a long while before the bathroom door opened again and the light switched off. Mac lay still until Chase climbed into bed and pressed against him. With a silent sigh of relief, Mac gathered Chase in his arms. "I'm here for you," he reminded Chase.

Chase kissed Mac's neck. "It was awful. I've never hurt someone so much in my life, and I never want to go through that again."

Mac rubbed a hand up and down Chase's back. "I know it was hard, but Benny's just starting his adult life. It's better that he start it with the truth."

"I'm not so sure," Chase mumbled.

Mac rolled to his back, pulling Chase with him. He waited until Chase's head settled on his chest before speaking. "My dad was in a bike club, so as you can imagine, I was expected to grow up and join the club as well. Coming out to a man like that wasn't possible, so I did my best to be the son he expected me to be. Janice, my ex-wife, was a good friend of mine in high school." He took a deep breath. Few people knew his story because it wasn't one he was particularly proud of. "I was experimenting with Skeet by then and knew I was one hundred percent gay, but I also loved and respected my dad enough to keep it a secret. Janice didn't know about me and Skeet and when she surprised me one day by kissing me, I knew she would be the one to help me fool everyone. She got pregnant when we were seniors in high school, and my dad ordered me to marry her."

Chase kissed Mac's chest.

"I lived a lie for eight years because I was afraid to tell the truth about the way I felt. It wasn't until I survived a serious motorcycle accident that no one should've walked away from that I knew I'd been given a second chance at life." Mac brushed his knuckles against Chase's cheek. "It took eight years and almost dying before I could do what you did tonight, so don't be too hard on yourself."

Chase scooted up in bed until his head rested on Mac's pillow. He trailed his fingers over the scars on Mac's shoulder. "Do you ever regret it?"

Mac swallowed the lump of emotion that threatened to choke him. "I miss my son, but I don't regret it."

They settled into silence and Mac wondered if Chase had fallen asleep. He rolled to his side to get closer to Chase.

"Do you and Skeet still mess around?" Chase asked, surprising Mac.

Mac sucked Chase's earlobe into his mouth. "No. Skeet and I want different things out of life. We haven't been lovers for years."

"But you're still friends," Chase murmured.

"He's my best friend," Mac acknowledged.

"I told Benny I wanted to be friends again, and he said he couldn't do it."

Mac gathered Chase in his arms. "Give him some time. He might change his mind." Although he'd said it, there was a part of him that didn't like the idea of Chase hanging out with Benny again. The relationship he'd had with Skeet was different. They had sex, sure, but they'd never been in love.

Chase kissed Mac's shoulder. "I'm glad you didn't die in the wreck."

"Yeah," Mac agreed. The accident had been horrific and Mac had been forced to take numerous hours of classes to go along with the DUI that was now on his record. He hadn't minded the fines or the classes. In his eyes, he'd gotten off damn lucky that he hadn't hurt someone else. Evidently, God watched over drunk morons.

* * * *

Chase stood next to his mom's car and waited for Mac to park the rental they'd picked up an hour earlier. He couldn't wait to get Mac's initial impression of Cattle Valley. The drive from Sheridan was beautiful, in his opinion, and he hoped Mac thought so, too. Why it was important to him, Chase didn't know, but it was. The day had started perfect, with early morning sex, but once they were out of bed, Mac had noticed the bruises on Chase's arms and the one on his chest. Mac had been furious and had threatened to call the police. It had taken Chase a long time to talk his lover down, so he hoped the drive further calmed Mac's temper.

Mac climbed out of the sedan and smiled at Chase. "You were right."

"Wait until you see the rest of the town." Chase entered the side door of Gill's. "Gill?"

"Yeah," Gill, the huge ex-football player appeared from a small office located between the garage and the gas station.

"Thanks for towing Mac's truck so early," Chase said, gesturing to Mac, who had wandered off toward the battered pickup.

Gill's gaze went from Chase to Mac. "I've ordered the glass and headlights, but it'll probably be tomorrow before they come in. The driver's door is going to take a little longer, so you might want to wait and have that fixed when you get back to Idaho."

"The insurance adjuster call you?" Mac asked. He had a scowl on his face and his arms crossed over his chest.

"Yeah. It's all taken care of on this end," Gill replied.

Mac walked around to the driver's side and winced.

Chase held his breath. Mac had been very forgiving when the damage happened, but Chase wasn't sure it would last once he saw the truck. He prayed it wouldn't remind Mac of the bruising.

Mac returned from inspecting the pickup to stand beside Chase. "I think you're right about the door. I'll take it to the dealership once we get home." He held out his hand to Gill. "I appreciate you getting right on it. Chase needs to get back to classes as soon as he can."

Gill shook Mac's hand. "Not a problem. Other than ordering the glass, there's not much I can do until it comes in. I've got your number, so I'll give you a call as soon as it's road ready."

"Thank you." Mac settled a hand low on Chase's back. "You ready?"

Chase nodded. He was uneasy with the public declaration in a town that loved Benny so much. He looked to Gill, praying the man wouldn't comment on the way he'd dumped Benny for Mac.

Gill eyed Chase for a moment. "I heard you had a hell of a season this year."

"Yeah," Chase answered. Gill had been one of Chase's biggest supporters when he'd decided to continue to play football as an openly gay man. "You should come to a game next year."

Gill nodded. "I'd like that." He grinned. "You planning to stop at the bakery?"

Smiling, Chase rubbed his stomach. "Can't come through town without getting my fill of cinnamon rolls."

"You got that right." Gill's phone began to ring, drawing him back toward the office. "I'll call ya."

"Thanks again," Mac said, leading Chase out the door.

Once outside, Chase pulled Mac's head down for a quick kiss. "Okay, I have to know. After seeing the truck, have you changed your mind about pressing charges?"

"No. I told you last night, the truck isn't important." Mac gave Chase another kiss. "I'm still not happy about the bruises, though."

Chase hadn't told Mac about getting tackled since Benny had managed to stop himself before any punches had been thrown. The bruising was regrettable, but it could have been so much worse. "I need to run by the bakery to load up on a few things. Then we'll drop Mom's car off, and I'll show you the rest of the town."

* * * *

Mac polished off his second cinnamon roll. "Damn, those are good."

"Told ya." Chase took a drink of milk.

Gwen came into the room. "Chase, while you're here, would you mind looking at the sink in the bathroom? I think it needs a new washer or something."

Chase grinned at Mac. "I wasn't lying when I said there's always something for me to fix around here." He stood and stretched his arms over his head. "Is the toolbox still in the coat closet?"

"It is if you put it back last time you used it," Gwen said, pouring a cup of coffee.

"You know I always put things away," Chase mumbled, heading out of the kitchen.

"Yeah, right." Gwen rolled her eyes and took a seat across from Mac.

Mac had spoken briefly with Chase's mother on the phone and again when they'd arrived thirty minutes earlier, but he had a feeling Gwen wanted to speak to him without Chase around. It didn't bother him. He'd want the same thing if he was her. "Ask me anything you want," he said, easing the way for her as he took a donut out of the box.

"How old are you?"

"Thirty-four. I'll be thirty-five in April," he answered honestly.

Gwen bit her lip. "I don't mean to be an ogre, but I worry about Chase. It was different when he was with Benny because he didn't have that distraction while at school." She chose an apple-cider cake donut from the box. "He has to get good grades to keep his scholarship, so his schoolwork is very important."

Mac retrieved the coffee pot and refilled his cup. "I completely agree with you. I don't want to take over Chase's life. I just want to share some of it with him. I know we've only known each other for a few weeks, but the time we've spent together has been some of the best of my life." He couldn't believe he was being so forthright with Gwen, but he'd spent a lifetime hiding what he really wanted.

Sighing, Gwen set the half-eaten donut on her plate. "I'm afraid he'll fall in love with you."

Mac wasn't in love with Chase, but he already cared a great deal for him. If they continued to see each other, he could very well see them falling in love eventually. He wondered if Gwen's concerns were due to Mac's age or something else. "If you're worried that I'm some kind of player, don't. I can count the number of male partners I've had on one hand."

"No, it's not that." Gwen leaned on the table and stared into Mac's eyes. "This thing with Benny has done some damage to Chase whether he'll admit that to you or not. Two heartbreaks this early in his life could cause permanent damage, and I don't want him to end up like me."

Mac reached across the table and squeezed Gwen's hand. "I have no plans to hurt him, but I hear what you're saying, and I promise we'll take it slow."

"Okay." Gwen removed her hand from Mac's and settled it in her lap.

"Hey, Mom," Chase said, entering the kitchen. "I think that faucet's shot. I'd run up and get a new one, but I was eyed enough at the bakery this morning. Would you mind?"

"Sure." Gwen stood and retrieved her purse. "What kind do I get?"

"The brand doesn't really matter. Just make sure you get one with separate hot and cold handles." Chase reached into his pocket and pulled out two twenties. "I think that should be enough."

"I don't need your money, Chase," Gwen argued as she put on her coat.

"Take it." Chase stuffed the bills in her pocket.

Gwen scowled but didn't hand the money back. "Do you need anything else while I'm out?"

"No. We're good." Chase waited until his mom left before turning to grin at Mac. "Did she give you the third degree?"

Mac shrugged. "She's your mom. She worries about you."

Chase straddled Mac's lap and draped his arms over Mac's shoulders. "Well, I'm sorry if she said anything inappropriate."

"She didn't." Mac wrapped his arms around Chase and pulled him closer. He'd planned to ask Chase to quit his job at the bar, but it was obvious Chase needed the work. It would be nice if he had the business to offer Chase a job at the shop, but there was no way he could afford to pay Chase what he made at Clean Slate.

"What?" Chase asked, swiveling his hips to grind his ass against Mac's cock.

"I don't want you to go out with anyone else," Mac stated. "I know you must get hundreds of offers a week, but I'm not into that. Going to the bar every night that you're working isn't my idea of a good time, so I need to be able to trust you."

"You don't have to worry about me. Of course, I'd like it if you came up to keep me company once in a while. The first half of the week is always slow." Chase gave Mac a soft kiss. "And I'll always have either Friday or Saturday off, so we can still hang out then."

It was obvious a relationship with Chase wouldn't be easy. Between school, homework and waiting tables, he wasn't sure there'd be much of Chase's time left. "What happens during football season?"

"I can't work during football season. Reid already knows that."

Mac nodded. "Why don't you talk to Reid and see if he can schedule you for Friday nights? That way you can spend the rest of the weekend at my place. During football season, we'll have to figure out something else."

Grinning, Chase kissed Mac again. "You think you'll still be interested in me next fall?"

Mac squeezed Chase's ass. "Why wouldn't I be?"

Chase shrugged. "I know I don't have an easy schedule to work around. It's never bothered me before because I haven't had anyone I wanted to spend time with, but I want to spend time with you." He reached between them and started to unbutton Mac's jeans.

Mac stilled Chase's hands and shook his head. "Not here."

"Mom'll probably be gone another ten or fifteen minutes."

"Doesn't matter. She's your mom, and so far, she's been nice to me. I'm not going to ruin that for ten minutes of fun." Mac sucked Chase's bottom lip into his mouth before releasing it. "We can head back to the hotel after dinner, and you'll have me all to yourself."

"Mmmm, I like that idea."

* * * *

Chase gave Mac a deep kiss in the parking lot of BK House. He wished he could go home with Mac, but without a car, he'd have no way to get to class in the morning. "I'm so used to sleeping with you, it's going to be weird having a bed to myself."

Mac chuckled. "Maybe you'll actually get some sleep for a change."

"Thanks for going with me, and for not being pissed about your truck." Chase pulled away and opened the passenger door before he could beg Mac to take him to the farmhouse.

Mac pulled Chase against him before he could get out of the pickup. "I should be the one thanking you. The last few days have opened my eyes to what's been missing in my life."

"Yeah? What's that, a smart-ass quarterback with an angry ex-boyfriend?" Chase opened his mouth to Mac's kiss, tasting a combination of Mountain Dew and road-trip junk food. It was the perfect ending to the trip.

"Just you. This," Mac added, releasing Chase. "Go study and call me before you go to sleep."

Chase smiled and grabbed his small suitcase from the backseat. "Will do." He climbed out of the truck, full of hope. "Tomorrow's Wednesday. Slow day and I have to work. I also have late classes on Thursday, so if you want, you could take me to your house after work." He shrugged. "No pressure."

Mac chuckled. "I'll be there."

Satisfied that he'd see Mac soon, Chase carried his suitcase into the dorm. It was only ten after nine, and he found Locky and Becket in the game room snuggled on the couch, watching TV. "Honey, I'm home," Chase called.

Locky unwound himself from Becket before getting to his feet. "I'm glad."

The worried expression on Locky's face alarmed Chase. "What's going on?"

"Remember how Rusty shut down after his parents died?" Locky asked. "Well, it's happened again.

Adam and Manuel brought him home on Sunday, and Rusty hasn't been out of your room since."

"Shit!" Chase had been so caught up in his own problems, he'd completely forgotten Rusty was most likely going through his own hell. "Okay. Thanks for the heads-up."

Chase left the game room and climbed the stairs. He strode down the hallway before stopping in front of his room. Knocking softly, he waited a minute before entering.

Rusty was stretched out on his bed with a book in his hand.

Chase dropped his suitcase in front of his closet. At least it seemed Rusty was reading for pleasure instead of studying. "How're you doing?" he asked, sitting on his bed.

"I'm fine," Rusty replied without looking away from his book.

Chase knew that wasn't the case but he wasn't sure whether or not he had the right to call his roommate on the lie. "Ribs okay?"

"Healing."

Chase slid off his bed and moved to kneel beside Rusty's. When Rusty cried out and quickly moved to press himself against the wall, Chase stopped. "Christ, Rusty." He dropped his hands. "I'm not going to hurt you."

It took a moment for Rusty to answer. "I know. I'm just jumpy lately."

"Yeah. I was like that for months after we left Seattle." Chase gestured to the bed. "Mind if I lay with you for a few minutes?"

Rusty closed his book. "I thought you had a boyfriend?"

Chase chuckled. "I do, but I'm not going to try anything. I used to sneak into my mom's room when I couldn't sleep. Even though I was probably stronger at the time, it made me feel safe." It was probably a stupid idea. He started to move back to his own bed, when Rusty cleared his throat.

"Maybe for a few minutes," Rusty mumbled.

"Cool." Chase kicked his shoes off before lying on his side next to Rusty. The bruises on Rusty's pale face were dark purple, but the swelling was down. "So what're you reading?"

Rusty held his book up.

"*Lord of the Flies*? Depressing much?" Chase had an idea of why Rusty was reading the story of children turning on each other, but he didn't voice it.

"It's better than the movie," Rusty said, defending his choice of books.

"Yeah." Chase blew out a breath. He'd been on the road for over fourteen hours. They'd gotten an early start, but bad weather in western Wyoming had put them behind schedule. "God, I'm tired."

"You did it?" Rusty asked, reaching over Chase to drop the mangled paperback on the floor.

"Yeah, and it didn't go like I'd hoped. Benny trashed Mac's truck. At first he was sad, but that quickly moved to uncontrollable rage." Chase sighed as his eyes drifted shut. "The worst part was how great Mac was about everything. I think I'm in trouble with him," he managed to say before drifting off

.

Chapter Six

Every time I think of you with him I want to puke!

Chase deleted the text as soon as he read it. It had been three weeks since he'd broken things off with Benny, and the texts still continued. He needed to block Benny's calls and texts, but he kept hoping the once sweet man would get over the anger. It sure as hell wasn't the way he'd wanted things to end between them.

"Problem?" Zeke asked.

Chase shoved his phone into his apron before lifting the tray of drinks. "Just a text from my ex."

Zeke leaned on the bar. "So how're things going with the new guy?"

"Good. I only get to see him a couple times a week, but it's good." It was more than good, but Zeke didn't need to know Chase lived for the snatches of time he and Mac were together.

"Is he going to be here tonight?" Zeke asked.

Chase shook his head. "I don't think so. Mac's caught that bug that's going around." It sucked that he didn't have a way to get to Mac's without Mac picking him up. He'd been looking for a cheap car online, but couldn't decide if a car was worth raiding his savings.

"Reid wants all staff to be walked out by either Holt or Jude. One of our customers reported seeing a group of men across the street a few nights ago. Fuckers don't even have enough balls to show their faces."

"Yeah," Chase agreed. According to Rusty, the men who had attacked him had worn ski masks. The fact that the men were out there somewhere, eager to beat someone else, made him sick. "I have to catch the bus at midnight. It's the last one for the night."

"I thought Wyatt usually dropped you off when you work late," Zeke said.

"Evidently, Wyatt's got a hot date. I told him I'd take the bus."

Zeke eyed Chase for a moment. "Let me talk to Reid."

"Don't worry about it. I'm used to the bus." Chase carried the heavy tray to a table of celebrating hunks. He knew some of them because they'd played football before graduating. While setting the drinks in front of the appropriate men, he caught snatches of conversation.

"To Demitri, the sexiest forty-year-old on the planet," Aaron Billings, the college's soccer coach toasted.

"Is it your birthday?" Chase asked, setting the last drink down.

"Yep, my baby brother is officially an old man," a handsome dark-haired man replied.

"Shut up, Theron," Demitri growled, ruining the warning with a wicked grin.

Chase left the table on a mission. He ducked into the kitchen to speak to Raul. "We've got a birthday out here. Can you fix me up one of those chocolate lava cakes with a candle?"

"Sure. Give me three minutes."

Tables caught up, Chase decided to use the time to check in with Mac. He dug his phone out of his pocket, grateful to see no more messages from Benny, and called Mac.

After the fourth ring, the phone picked up. "Hello?"

"Oh, Mac, you sound like shit." Chase paced back and forth in front of the time clock.

"I feel worse than I sound."

Chase retrieved his order pad and a pen from his apron. "What's your address?"

It took a few moments, but eventually Mac rattled it off between bouts of coughing. "Why do you need it?" Mac asked.

"Because I'm coming out," Chase replied.

"No, I'll make you sick."

"If I get sick I get sick. I live in a dorm full of hacking idiots right now, and if I'm going to get it, I'd rather get it from you." There were only a few who hadn't caught the virus. Luckily, he and Rusty were two of them. Chase figured he must have a strong immune system, and Rusty had barely left their room in the weeks since the attack. Instead, Rusty did his homework in the room and gave it to Chase to deliver or emailed it to his professors.

"I have another hour left of my shift, but I'll be over after that. Just unlock your front door sometime between now and then," Chase instructed.

Raul motioned to Chase that the dessert was ready.

"Gotta go." Chase hung up before Mac could protest further. He prayed the miniature birthday cake would help garner enough tips to take a taxi.

* * * *

Chase let himself into Mac's farmhouse. Once he'd mentioned to Raul how sick Mac was, Raul had made a batch of soup that he claimed would heal a man on his deathbed. The stuff smelled like vegetables and hot sauce, but Raul had taken the time to make it, so Chase hoped it worked.

After a quick walkthrough of the downstairs, Chase left the soup in the refrigerator before making his way to Mac's bedroom on the second floor. Mac had the bedside lamp turned on but was sound asleep, huddled under a mountain of quilts.

Chase grabbed the small trashcan out of the bathroom and gathered the pile of tissues from off the table at Mac's side. "Poor baby," he whispered.

Mac's bloodshot eyes opened. "Hey."

Chase sat on the mattress. "How're you doing?" He put the back of his hand to Mac's forehead and couldn't believe how hot Mac was. "Jesus, Mac, you're burnin' up." He jumped up and strode to the bathroom. "Do you think you should go to the emergency room?" he asked, running cold water over a washcloth.

"I'll be fine in a few days," Mac mumbled.

Chase pressed the washcloth to Mac's forehead. "I'm going to call Mom."

"You don't need to do that."

Yeah he did. Chase wanted to take care of Mac, but didn't know the first thing about how to do it. He pulled out his phone and called home. A quick glance at the clock told him it was almost one.

"Chase?" Gwen answered, her voice full of worry.

"Hey, Mom. Mac's really sick, and I don't know what to do." Chase picked up the washcloth and refolded it before placing it back on Mac's forehead.

"Is it that flu that's going around?" Gwen asked.

"I guess so. I just got here, and he's burning up. I have a cool washcloth on his forehead, but what else do I do?" Chase stared at Mac who had already gone back to sleep.

"Make sure he's getting plenty of fluids and taking something to bring the fever down. If he can't keep the water down, break up some ice and feed it to him. Other than that, just try to make him comfortable. If his temperature gets too high, you might need to get him into a cool bath."

"It tears me up to see him like this and not be able to help him." Chase leaned down and kissed Mac's cheek.

Gwen sighed. "It comes with loving someone. I thought you were going to take your relationship with Mac slow."

"We *are* taking it slow." Chase walked out of the bedroom and into the hall. "I only see him a few days a week. I can't help it if he's so damn wonderful I'm falling for him."

"Promise me that if things don't work out, you won't give up on falling in love with someone else."

In the five weeks since he'd met Mac, it hadn't mattered whether Chase was in class or at work, Mac was all that he thought about. When they weren't together, Chase wondered what Mac was doing, if he was happy or lonely, working on a bike or taking a nap in the backroom of the shop. Yes, he supposed he had fallen in love, despite his desire to take things slow.

"I don't want to talk about that, Mom. I'm sorry I called so late. I'm worried, and I didn't know what to do. I'll try to get him to drink something and keep the bath in mind." Chase hated to hang up on his mom, but he didn't want to hear any more about going on after things with Mac ended. "I love you. I'll talk to you later."

"Be careful," Gwen said before Chase hung up.

Scowling, Chase turned the phone off. *Fluids.* He ducked back into the bedroom to check for a glass beside Mac's bed.

"I thought you left," Mac said.

"Nope. I called Mom." Chase leaned over and kissed Mac's temple. "She told me to feed you ice chips."

"She did?" Mac's eyes drifted closed again. "Are you gonna do that?"

Staring down at Mac, Chase knew all he wanted was to take care of him. "Yeah."

* * * *

Mac held tight to the banister as he made his way down the stairs. He wasn't over the flu by a long shot, but staring at the four walls in his bedroom was driving him batshit crazy. He found Chase at the kitchen table doing his homework. Without making a sound, he leaned heavily against the counter and watched Chase work.

For two days, Chase had spent every spare moment taking care of him, and Mac had let him because it felt good to be taken care of for a change. *Hell.* Chase looked damn good at his table. He wished he felt better.

Chase glanced up from his computer. "Did you call me?" He jumped up and pulled out a chair for Mac. "What can I get you? I still have some of that soup."

Mac shook his head. "No, no more soup." He eased down into the chair. "What're you working on?"

"Well, I'm supposed to be writing a paper on the design and construction of the Washington Monument, but I got sidetracked looking for a cheap car." Chase closed his laptop. "How're you feeling?"

Mac rested his head on the cool surface of the table. "Like shit, but I missed you."

Chase grinned. "You have no idea how much I want to kiss you right now."

"You have no idea how much I want that, too." Mac tapped the laptop. "So, did you find a car?"

Chase sighed and dropped his head back. "No and it's so frustrating. Everything I can afford looks like it'll fall apart as soon as I get it out on the highway."

Mac opened the laptop. "Let me help you." He scrolled through the listings. "Are you looking for anything in particular?"

"We don't have to do this now. You should probably go back to bed." Chase felt Mac's forehead. "You've still got a slight fever."

Mac knew there was no arguing with his sexy nursemaid. "Why don't we both go upstairs and we can look at these in bed?" he offered.

"Okay, but just for a little while. I really do need to finish that damn paper." Chase unplugged the laptop. "You head up, and I'll grab some bottles of water."

Mac got to his feet. On his way out of the kitchen, he stopped in front of Chase. "I like you in my house."

Chase kissed Mac's neck. "Go on. You look like you're about to fall down."

Mac didn't deny it. The flu was kicking his ass.

On the way to his bedroom, Mac noticed Chase had vacuumed the living room area rug and if he wasn't mistaken, Chase had also dusted. Damn, he was impressed. He wasn't a slob by any stretch of the imagination, but dust wasn't something he cared about enough to take care of. Evidently Chase did though. He made a mental note to dust more often as he made his way up the stairs.

Mac was almost to the top of the steps when Chase ran passed him. "Slowpoke," Chase called, bouncing up and down on the landing.

"I'll poke ya," Mac grumbled, but by the time he reached the top, he was panting. He rested his hand against the newel post. "I'll have to take a rain check on the poking."

Chase's arm wrapped around Mac's waist. "You're still sick. Next time you miss me, call me. You know I'll come running."

Mac did. Goddamn, Chase was the sexiest, most attentive lover he'd ever had, and he wanted nothing more than to keep him. "I'm okay now," he said when Chase helped him into bed.

Chase undressed down to his underwear and slid under the covers. "You sure you're up to this? We can always look at cars later."

Mac opened one of the bottles of water and drank half of it in one gulp. "I told you, I'm okay. Just show me the fucking cars," he grumbled.

Chase bit his bottom lip but didn't say anything. Instead, he climbed out of bed before disappearing into the bathroom.

Mac wiped a hand over his face. He shouldn't have snapped like that. It wasn't Chase's fault he felt like shit. Chase had been nothing but patient with him.

"Aw, hell." He threw back the blankets and got out of bed.

"Babe?" Mac called through the closed door. "I'm sorry."

Chase opened the door. "No, I'm sorry I ran away like that. I know you don't feel well, and I didn't want to snap back at you."

Mac knew it was time he and Chase had a talk. "Let's go to bed."

As soon as they were back under the covers, Mac pulled Chase against him. "I know you're not comfortable with arguments, but we're going to have them. There'll be times I get pissed. There'll be times you get pissed. If this is going to work between us, we have to learn to work it out."

"I can work it out, but I don't think I'll ever be able to fight back."

Mac moved to lean his back against the headboard. He resettled Chase in his arms and rubbed the whiskers on his chin against the top of Chase's blond head. How did he make the younger man understand how important it was to stand up for himself? Even on a good day, Mac knew he could be an asshole. He'd grown up in a fairly hostile environment where men fought with their words and fists, and he wasn't used to censoring himself. Sure, he could do it most of the time, but there would be occasions when his temper and mouth got the better of him. It was those moments he needed to prepare Chase for because having Chase walk away from him after one argument wasn't an option he wanted to think about. Maybe it was time to lay it all out on the table.

"You're angry with me," Chase said, kissing the tattoo on Mac's chest.

"No, frustrated," Mac answered. "I'm falling in love with you, but I know it won't work between us with things the way they are."

Chase sat up and stared at Mac. "I feel the same way, so I know we can make it work."

Mac shook his head. "Benny's the only man you've ever loved before we got together, and you've told me more than once how sweet Benny is. Yet, you're here with me. I'm not sweet. I grew up in a house of hell-raisers. Most importantly, I'm not like your father. I can have an argument without resorting to violence, and the sooner you understand that, the sooner we can move forward together. Until that happens, I don't see a future for us."

"You're breaking up with me?"

"No. I'm not that stupid, but I can't make plans for tomorrow when I don't know if you'll be there." Mac gestured to the laptop. "I was going to suggest we find something cheap, and I could help you fix it up. Now, I'm not sure if that's a good idea."

Chase rubbed his eyes with the heels of his hands. "So, let me get this straight. Because we don't fight, you're worried we won't last? That's fucked up."

Mac tried hard not to grin. He was baiting Chase to see if he could get him angry, and it seemed to be working. "Maybe, but since you refuse to argue about anything, I guess that means I can have my way in anything I want."

"Why're you being such a dick?" Chase asked, his face flushed with anger.

Sick or not, Mac couldn't help but grab Chase's face and kiss him. He pulled back and smiled. "It's a start."

* * * *

"Professor Ryan wants you to call him," Chase told Rusty as he walked into the dorm room.

"Why? Didn't you hand in my project?" Rusty spun around in his desk chair and stared at Chase.

"Of course I did, but you've got an exam on Friday, and Ryan said you can't do that in your room. He wants you to call him to make arrangements." Chase couldn't figure out what was going on between Rusty and the professors. Rusty had willingly gone home with Adam and Manuel on the night of the attack, but hadn't seen either of the men since they'd brought him back to the dorm two days later.

"If it matters, Professor Ryan seems really worried about you," Chase added when Rusty didn't reply.

Rusty turned back to his computer. "I'll send him an email."

Groaning at his stubborn roommate, Chase threw himself on his bed. Since the beating, every night Chase wasn't with Mac, he'd spent with his bed shoved next to Rusty's. Moving his bed back and forth was getting tiresome, but on the one night he'd said no, Chase didn't think Rusty had slept a wink. He wondered what Rusty did when he slept at Mac's. "Maybe you should talk to Becket."

"What?" Rusty asked without turning around.

"You seem to be having a hard time lately, and I think Becket could probably either help you with it or give you the name of someone who could."

"I don't need help," Rusty denied. "If you don't want to take my homework to my professors, just tell me."

Although it was a pain in the ass to make the rounds of the science building every day, Chase wanted to be there for his friend. "I didn't say I minded. I'm worried about you. That's all," he added.

Rusty's sigh ended with a loud groan. He finally looked at Chase. "Growing up, the kids at my school called me Icky, and every day I was bullied. I kept telling myself it would stop once I grew up and got away from those people. That finally, I wouldn't have to constantly look over my shoulder." He choked out a bitter laugh. "I realize now that I'm destined to look over my shoulder for the rest of my life." Tears filled the big green eyes behind his glasses. "It's one more reminder that I don't fit in anywhere."

"That's bullshit. Everyone in this dorm would go to the mat for you." Chase sat up. Time for some tough love, he thought. "By hiding out in here, you're letting the bullies win. Maybe it's time you did something to take your life back."

"Like what?" Rusty gestured to himself. "I'm not built like you. I'm a skinny ginger with glasses. Unless I walk around campus wielding a gun, no one's ever going to be intimidated by me enough to leave me alone."

Chase shrugged, unsure how to reply. Rusty had a good point. Where Chase saw a cute guy with a boyish face, others saw a target. "Maybe you need to look into self-defense classes. If a woman can learn enough to fight off an attacker, why couldn't you?"

"That's what Manuel said," Rusty mumbled.

The way Rusty said Professor Corto Delgado's name made Chase curious. "What's going on there? You trusted them then suddenly you don't even want to talk to them on the phone. Did they hurt you or something?"

Rusty immediately shut down. "I don't want to talk about it."

Rusty's reaction to the question said more to Chase than words ever could. "If they hurt you, you need to tell someone," he ground out, hands fisted.

"They didn't hurt me. Seriously, just drop it," Rusty snapped.

Determined to get answers, Chase jumped off the bed. "If you don't want to talk to me, fine, I'll go ask them."

"Wait!" Rusty was out of his chair and in front of the door before Chase could grab his coat. "I like them. Like, really like them," Rusty admitted. "I made a fool out of myself when I stayed with them, and I can't bring myself to talk to either of them."

Chase caught Rusty's meaning and grinned. "Did a three-way happen?"

"No!" Rusty exclaimed, appearing insulted by the suggestion. He grabbed Chase's arms. "Please. I'm begging you to just drop it."

Knowing the sexy professors hadn't hurt Rusty, Chase decided to give into Rusty's pleas. "Okay, but you need to do something, man. Change classes or whatever. Hell, I'll start walking you to class if that's what it takes, but you have got to get out of this fucking room."

"I'll think about it if you promise not to talk to Adam or Manuel about it."

"You show up for all your tests, and I'll keep my mouth shut." Chase stuck out his hand. "Deal?"

After a few moments, Rusty shook Chase's hand. "Deal."

* * * *

Mac was installing a new water pump on Chase's two-thousand-six Honda Civic, when the shop phone rang. "Shit." He balanced the part against the engine block before racing to the wall-mounted phone. "Mac's," he answered.

There was a moment of silence before the caller spoke. "Dad?"

Mac gripped the phone tighter. "Jackson?"

"Did you send me a Christmas present?" Jackson asked.

Mac carried the phone to his desk and sat down heavily. "Yeah. I'm glad you kept it, son."

"I found it outside in the trashcan. I—I dug it out and read the card." Jackson's breath hitched. "I didn't know that you still thought about me."

"Every day," Mac said. "I love you. I can't tell you how many times I've wanted to apologize for what happened. I never meant for you to overhear me talking to your mom that day."

"I was mad for a long time, but once I got older, I started really thinking about it, and I wanted to talk to you, too, but Mom said she didn't know where you were."

Fuckin' bitch. Mac was furious, but tried to tamp down his rage for Jackson's sake. "I'm sorry she did that to you. Every time I tried to call, she told me you didn't want to speak to me."

"I didn't know," Jackson said. "It took a while, but once I started snooping in Mom's stuff, I found your number. I need you to know that I'm still not comfortable having a gay dad, but I'm working on it. Butch is okay, but the best memories I have happened with you."

"Can I see you?" Mac would file court papers tomorrow to fight for the right to see his only son.

"I'm not really there yet, but I'd like it if we could talk and get to know each other again." Jackson cleared his throat. "I'm not saying that to hurt you or anything."

"I know, and I'm grateful for whatever you can give." Mac ran a hand down his chin, stopping to tug the whiskers in an effort to make sure he wasn't dreaming. "I can't tell you how happy I am that you even want to talk to me."

"I need to work some stuff out with Mom, but maybe we could set up a schedule to talk."

"I'd like that," Mac agreed. "Get a pen, and I'll give you my cell phone number."

"Isn't that what I called?" Jackson asked.

"No, you called my shop. I don't have anything like what I had in LA, but I've got another custom bike shop. It suits me." Mac glanced around. Truth was, he liked the smaller shop better.

"Cool. Hang on."

Mac heard Jackson shuffling papers and opening drawers.

"Okay. I'm ready," Jackson said.

Mac rattled off his cell number. "You want my address?"

"Sure, then I'll give you my digits."

After Mac gave his address, he wrote down Jackson's number. It would be so nice to call Jackson without worrying that Janice would answer. "Got it."

"I'd better go, but I'll try to call again on Sunday if that's okay."

"Call me anytime day or night. I'll always be here for you." Mac hoped he wasn't laying it on too thick, but it took every ounce of his self-control not to demand to see Jackson. "I love you, son."

"Thanks, Dad."

Long after Jackson had hung up, Mac continued to stare at the phone. He hadn't planned to go to the bar to see Chase, Friday nights were awful at Clean Slate, but he was in such a good mood that he couldn't wait to share the news with the man he loved.

* * * *

Chase gave Zeke his drink order for table twelve. He'd been working with Zeke for a few days on his dance moves, something he was still unsure about. The problem was, the car had taken a chunk out of his savings, and if that weren't bad enough, Mac had a whole list of parts he wanted to replace on the vehicle before he'd let Chase drive it.

"What if I make a fool of myself?" Chase glanced at the clock over the bar. Less than ten minutes until Zeke's usual Friday and Saturday night bar-dancing shtick began.

Zeke chuckled. "You've got the moves. You just need to lose the nerves. Look around, half these assholes are drunk. You could get up and do the hokey pokey and they'd drool."

"Okay, but I'm only going to do one dance. Mac bought a water pump today that I need to pay him back for." Chase looked down at himself. He'd worn the low-rise jeans he'd sworn he'd never go out in public in and a tight white Clean Slate T-shirt.

"Here. Deliver these, and I'll get the music queued up."

Chase did his best to smile as he delivered the drinks. His stomach was churning at the thought of shaking his ass in front of a roomful of people, drunk or not.

* * * *

Mac bumped Holt's fist with his own. "How's it going tonight?"

Holt shook his head and gestured over his shoulder. "Better for me than you."

Confused, Mac looked beyond Holt. Standing on the bar, Chase was facing the wall with his ass toward the crowd as he moved to the rhythm of the music.

"What the fuck is that!" Mac growled. One of the main reasons he didn't like the bar on Friday or Saturday nights was the show Zeke put on. He couldn't believe Chase was up there wiggling his ass for everyone to get hard over. Blood boiling, he knew if he didn't get out of there, he'd make a huge scene.

Chase swiveled his hips and started to turn around when his gaze met Mac's.

Mac shook his head and turned to leave. If Chase wanted to let other men look at him, he'd leave him to it. "Fuck!" He pushed through the door angrier than he had been in years. He knew he shouldn't have started something with someone who worked in a bar. Temptation would always be at Chase's fingertips, and no way in hell was Mac going to spend every night babysitting.

"Mac!" Chase yelled from behind him.

Mac spun around and faced Chase. "Do I look like a fucking schmuck to you? You think you can go behind my back and shake your ass for those fucking perverts, and I wouldn't find out!" he screamed. "How long, Chase? How long have you been going behind my back?"

"This was the first time," Chase said, reaching for Mac.

Mac knocked Chase's hands away. "The first time you danced or the first time I caught you? I wondered how you came up with the money to pay cash for that damn car."

"Fuck you!" Chase screamed, pushing hard against Mac's chest. "I bought that car so I could spend more time with you, you sonofabitch! I used the money that I've been saving for room and board next year, all because I didn't want to keep bothering you to give me a fucking ride. Then you want to make all these repairs, and I don't have the money for that shit, but I couldn't tell you no, so I had to make that money somehow, and I don't make enough just waiting tables!" His face red with anger, Chase pushed Mac again. "Damn you for making me feel like a slut," he snapped before turning back toward the club.

Mac was frozen to the spot for several moments, processing what had just happened. "Chase!" he called before Chase could get too far away.

Chase glanced over his shoulder. "What?" he spat out, obviously still angry.

"You did it," Mac declared. "I acted like an ass and you called me on it." He grinned. "I'm proud of you."

Chase charged Mac. "You did that on purpose?"

Mac grabbed Chase, pinning Chase's arms to his sides. "No, babe, that was real. When I saw you up there dancing, I wanted to tear the fucking place apart. I didn't expect you to come after me. I sure as hell didn't expect you to scream at me and try your best to push me around. I wasn't prepared for your reaction, but I fuckin' loved it." He took Chase's mouth in a deep kiss, thrusting his tongue inside. His hands were still shaking with a combination of anger and adrenaline, but his heart was soaring. He slid his hands down Chase's back to the waist of the low-rise jeans. Fuck, his man was sexy.

Chase pulled back, breaking the kiss. "You're a freak. You know that, right?"

"A freak you love?" Mac asked.

"A freak I don't want to live without." Chase sucked Mac's lower lip into his mouth. "Are you coming in until I get off? I promise, no more dancing."

Mac draped his arm around Chase's waist as they walked toward the bar. "You can dance for me later, and I'll tip you bigger than any of these cocksuckers."

Epilogue

"Move in," Mac said, thrusting his cock deep inside Chase. "The weekends aren't enough for me anymore."

Chase glanced over his shoulder. "You're such a romantic guy. I can't believe we're having this conversation while you're fucking me."

Mac frowned and pulled out of Chase's ass. "Fine. We won't fuck then."

Chase rolled to his back and hooked Mac's shoulders with his heels. "Oh, no you don't. You're not leaving me riding the edge like this."

Mac did not intend to leave either of them hanging, but he wanted an answer to his question. "I'm tired of living my life for the weekends when I want you every day."

"Fuck me, then we'll talk," Chase begged, lifting his ass off the bed.

"Nope. Either you want to or you don't." The longer Chase put him off, the lower Mac's spirits fell. He'd thought Chase would jump at the chance to be together fulltime. Had he misread the direction their relationship was headed?

"Of course I want to, ya big jackass, but maybe I want wine and roses with the question," Chase argued.

Mac stared down at Chase. He'd unleashed a monster. "I don't really know how to be romantic. I may be crass at times, but I do love you." He guided his cock back to Chase's hole and eased inside.

Chase ran a palm down Mac's chest and grinned. "I know you do, and I love you too. I was just bustin' your balls."

Mac pulled out before driving in hard and deep. "Just for that, I'm going to make you beg for it." He held Chase's wrists to the mattress so he couldn't touch himself.

"Not a problem," Chase replied. "I'll beg for you any day of the week."

"How about *every* day of the week?" Yeah, Mac liked the sound of that. He set a hard rhythm, promising himself he'd try to bring romance to their relationship. For him, working together on Chase's car was romantic, but evidently, he had it all wrong.

Chase tried to free his hands. "Come on, Mac, let me touch myself."

"Nope." Mac lowered himself enough to press against Chase's cock. "I want to be the reason you come."

Chase grinned. "You're always the reason I come."

"Prove it." Mac stared down at Chase. He swiveled his hips, grinding his pubic hair against Chase's cock.

"Oh shit!" Chase shouted, bucking up against Mac as he came.

"Yeah," Mac grunted, loving the way Chase's inner walls clenched around his cock. His orgasm rocked him to the core, bringing all his love to the forefront. He collapsed on top of Chase and buried his face against Chase's neck. "Stay with me," he whispered against Chase's skin.

"Yes," Chase answered back. "Always."

* * * *

Chase knocked on the front door of the bar and waited. He was scared to death that Reid was going to fire him. All day he'd tried to figure out what he'd done to warrant being called into work early, and he'd come up with absolutely nothing.

"Hey," Jude greeted, holding the door open. "Reid's in the kitchen."

"In the kitchen?" Chase asked. The time clocks were in the kitchen. Did Reid think he'd cheated on one of his timecards? He hadn't, but he knew Wyatt did on occasion, not that Chase would ever tell on his friend.

"Yeah." Jude locked the door. "Reid said for you to go on back when you got in."

"Okay." Chase started to take off his coat but stopped himself. If Reid was going to fire him, he'd just have to put it back on again. He passed by the bar and noticed that Zeke didn't make eye contact. *Shit, fuck, damn*, he strung the cuss words together in his head as he entered the kitchen.

Reid was standing in the middle of the prep area.

"You wanted to see me?" Chase swallowed around the lump of fear in his throat. *Shit. I am so fired.*

"Come with me. There's something I need to show you." Reid led the way toward the employee break room.

"Have I done something wrong?" Chase asked.

"I don't think so." Reid opened the door and stepped back. "After you," he said with a slight bow and flourish of his hand.

Chase took a hesitant step inside the room and almost fell over. Seated at the employee dining table was Mac, but the break room didn't look at all like it usually did. White linen, candles and a strand of hastily strung fairy lights decorated the room. "Mac?" He took another few steps into the room. "What's going on?"

The door closed behind Chase, leaving them alone.

"I wanted to surprise you," Mac said, getting to his feet. He drew a single rose from out of the vase on the table and held it out.

Chase would never tell Mac how weird he felt in that moment. He knew what Mac was trying to do, and he loved his big guy even more for the attempt, but what the hell? "Are we celebrating something?"

"Not really. I heard from Jackson last night, and he wants me to come down to LA for Spring Break. Since the last time I asked you an important question you told me you needed wine and roses..." Mac gestured to the table. "I thought I'd try my best to get it right this time."

Chase's heart squeezed. Despite the cheesy setting, Mac's heart was definitely in the right place. "What do you need to ask me?"

Mac pulled Chase's chair out and waited for him to sit down. "I want you to go with me to LA. I already talked to Reid and he said it's usually slow during Spring Break anyway, so he doesn't have a problem with it."

Chase watched as Mac sat in the chair next to him instead of at the opposite end of the table. "Are you sure you want me to go? Wouldn't you rather spend that time with Jackson?"

"Janice won't let Jackson spend the whole week with me, but she has agreed to several visits. But, it really isn't about Janice or Jackson. I want you to come with me, because I need you there," Mac explained.

Chase leaned across the table. "You're a romantic sonofabitch."

Mac gave Chase a deep kiss. "I try."

* * * *

"Maybe I should stay here," Chase offered. He felt guilty enough driving down to LA with Mac. The thought of showing up with Mac for his reunion with Jackson didn't feel right.

"I want you there." Mac crossed the hotel room to pull Chase into a tight embrace. "Jackson knows about you, and I need him to understand that he has to accept all of me, and that includes your place in my life."

"Does he know how young I am?" Chase asked. He didn't want the age difference between him and Mac to cause a problem.

"He knows you play football, so I'd assume so." Mac finished buttoning Chase's shirt for him. "So, what'd your mom say about this summer?"

"I already told you that she's fine with me moving in after the semester ends." It was Rusty that Chase hadn't told. He wasn't sure how his roommate was going to handle it. Although Rusty was better, he still refused to attend regular classes, only going in for exams. Rusty promised Chase he'd use the time off for Spring Break to get his head on straight.

"I know you did, but you didn't tell me what she actually said." Mac retrieved his wallet from the bedside table. "Does she think I'm trying to steal her baby?"

"Not at all." Chase checked his hair in the mirror before following Mac out the door. "She told me if I'd honestly found the real thing to hang on to it and enjoy every second we have together."

"I've always liked your mom." Mac kissed Chase's temple as they waited for the elevator.

"You should. She's closer to your age," Chase teased.

Mac slapped Chase's ass. "Smart ass."

Chase rested his head on Mac's shoulder as they rode down the elevator. Never had he hoped for the kind of relationship he had with Mac. He'd known the sexual chemistry was missing with Benny, but what he hadn't realized was how important it was to have the whole package. Sex was simply one component of his love for Mac. It went beyond sex or friendship.

It was living each day with someone who loved your flaws as much as they loved your attributes, and over the last several months, he'd grown to love every part of Mac. It was coming clean with yourself and those around you in order to find the true person you were always meant to be.

Yeah, Chase had it good, and he knew it.

About the Author

An avid reader for years, one day Carol Lynne decided to write her own brand of erotic romance. Carol juggles between being a full-time mother and a full-time writer. These days, you can usually find Carol either cleaning jelly out of the carpet or nestled in her favourite chair writing steamy love scenes.

Carol Lynne loves to hear from readers. You can find her contact information, website details and author profile page at http://www.totallybound.com.

Totally Bound Publishing

Home of Erotic Romance